In Search of Your Soul:

Discovering Your Inner Self,
Made in the Image of God

Copyright © 2019 by Dr. Richard Cheatham.

All rights reserved. No part of this book may be reproduced in any form or by any electronic or mechanical means, including information storage and retrieval systems, without permission in writing from the publisher, except by reviewers, who may quote brief passages in a review.

This publication contains the opinions and ideas of its author. It is intended to provide helpful and informative material on the subjects addressed in the publication.

The authors and publisher specifically disclaim all responsibility for any liability, loss, or risk, personal or otherwise, which is incurred as a consequence, directly or indirectly, of the use and application of any of the contents of this book.

ISBN: 978-1-948828-60-4   [Paperback Edition]
       978-1-948828-61-1   [eBook Edition]

Printed and bound in The United States of America.
Published by Access-Media Group
✉ *customer.service@access-mediagroup.com*

IN SEARCH
of Your *Soul*

*Discovering Your Inner Self,
Made in the Image of God*

Dr. Richard Cheatham

Acknowledgements

The decision to write this book rose from the many news accounts that caused an old timer like myself to realize this nation of today is not at all like the one I knew as a young person. Therefore, I thought it might be useful— to at least some— to share my understanding and offer some help.

In typical fashion, I offer the words of Tennyson: *"I am a part of all that I have met."* Wisdom is acquired slowly over the years, and it comes from our experiences. Everyone I have met and spent time with has, in some way, affected my understanding of myself and life in general. We all owe a debt of gratitude to those who shared some part of life's journey with us.

I have lived with these ideas for decades and, unfortunately began the writing with far too many assumptions about the readers' understanding of the issues. My friend, Jim Karlak, read the manuscripts carefully and thoughtfully, and called me on those assumptions. I am grateful for his assistance in making this book more intelligible than it otherwise might have been.

My daughters, their families, and some assorted friends have encouraged me along the way. I am grateful to them, for sometimes a writer begins to wonder whether or not she or he has anything of value to offer. However, the one I must acknowledge for her belief in me and her fine editorial eye is Diane, my wife. She has been my partner-in-ministry since we started.

Preface

The oldest Gospel, Mark, begins with Jesus saying *"The Kingdom of God is at hand. Repent and believe the good news."* This simple statement lays the foundation for all that follows. The problems for the typical Christian pilgrims are that they understand this in terms of the manner in which those words are understood today. A living language evolves over time and words change their meaning. Scripture was written for the people of that time and the language of that time must be understood in order to know the ideas being conveyed. Words also vary in meaning in different cultures. The term *kingdom*, for example, is understood as we in the United States understand the term *nation*. When people in Great Britain speak of the kingdom, their mind does not conjure up images of castles as it does for Americans. Rather, it simply means *nation* to them. The Kingdom of God simply means the People of God who live in relationship and obedience to God. Luke expressed it more clearly when Jesus responds to the Pharisees by saying, "The Kingdom is within you." (*Luke 17:21*). More importantly is the term translated as *repent*. It now implies bearing a sense of guilt. Evangelists call for people to repent and they come forward often weeping tears of remorse. Many pseudo Greek scholars will say it means *to change your mind or to turn around*. The Greek term is *metanoia*. *Meta* as in metamorphous or transformation of the body. *Nous* denotes the function of the mind. The first century understood the term to mean the transformation of the mind ("after careful thought" was implied*)*.

So, Jesus was announcing that the nation of God was at hand and if people transformed their thinking they could become a part of it. He then demonstrates how our minds could be transformed by loving obedience. I believe Jesus' call to repent was an invitation to become more in touch with our souls.

This is my attempt to strip away the religious jargon and symbolism, of traditional Christianity in order to explore those unknown qualities that comprise humanity. Traditional religious jargon such as "grace," "God's love," and "spirit-filled," may sound fine but they do not convey useful information for the earnest spiritual pilgrim. Early in my ministry I realized that most religious terms could be more clearly expressed in psychological terms. Psychology actually means the study of the soul. When I studied at the Jungian Institute in Zurich I realized that Jung actually was a very spiritual person. Once, when asked if he believed in God, his simple response was, "No, I do not believe in God ... I *know* God. The purpose of religion is not to worship God but to enter into relationship with God. I believe that, in using more secular terms, we can find the method for transforming our minds and then actually become a part of God's people. When that occurs, we may have the feeling of being born spiritually, losing our sense of loneliness and living more fully and purposefully.

Every culture has its religious language, stories, worldview and philosophies or theologies. Every culture draws from its traditions to create some system that will give security, meaning and hope to its people. Those who have made an in-depth study of the major world religions see the commonality. Far too many, lesser-educated people, believe their particular religion is the one true faith. In order to maintain their sense of security they close their minds to any other expression of faith, and in doing so, delay their own spiritual development.

DR. RICHARD CHEATHAM

Mark Schaefer, in his book, *The Certainty of Uncertainty*, notes that the church is in the business of marketing. He writes: *"The church, and indeed much of religion in general, has become the purveyor of yet another product in a saturated market of solutions. Faith, then, becomes one more product promising fulfillment, happiness and "unwavering bliss." (p.13)*

Essentially the message is that most activities are not fully satisfying and fall short of what is required for people to feel secure with meaningful and worthy lives. Also, none last beyond this lifetime, and leave us in limbo upon our death. They then offer the alternative of Jesus. "Just give yourself to Jesus and life will be better." "He is the way, the truth and the life," should be the slogan. Unfortunately, it was quickly distorted to "Jesus died for your sin." There is no biblical basis for this, but the idea was sneaked in through the backdoor by theologians unskilled in biblical interpretation. It actually contradicts the 18th chapter of Ezekiel, and is contrary to Jewish theology.

I wish to examine and explain the reasons why I believe a worthy, deeply-embedded faith is the only alternative to an otherwise wasted life. The individual's faith may be one that rejects anything that appears to be religious. What is critical is the underlying dynamics of that faith. As a practical matter, I often have found a greater sense of spiritual kinship with those of other faiths— and even those who overtly reject any faith— than I have with some members of my United Methodist Church— even some clergy. "*By your fruit, you shall be known.*" (not by the fertilizer [theology] that was spread on you)

In my last book, *Rediscovering Christianity*, I listed *the* primary rules by which I do my theology. I believe it was helpful for the reader, so I shall list them again:

1. Ockham's Razor. This simply means that the simplest answer is probably the correct answer. Rather than constructing a contorted explanation to explain a

process, the least complicated is the desired— and most likely— explanation.

2. My functional definition of truth is this: the hypothesis that successfully answers every question posed to it. If a question arises that cannot be answered by that hypothesis, then that understanding of truth is no longer functional. If a person chooses to deny the legitimate questions posed by this scientifically-oriented society, I assume that person has chosen to remain intentionally ignorant. Any discussion with that person will only prove to be frustrating— never fruitful.

3. Check the premises. Every decision we make is based upon at least one premise. Most of our premises are long-accepted, assumed truths. We begin our reasoning process unconsciously accepting certain long-held truths, and proceed from there. I have learned that many false conclusions are logically attained through this process. The old adage, "What goes up must come down," no longer is true in this day of space venturing. We now realize that it is possible to overcome the operational force of gravity that once made this an unquestionable truth. As you will read a bit further into this book, you will see that a few false premises are the root cause of the doctrine of Trinity. Without those, that doctrine no longer serves a purpose, but— at least in my estimation— interferes with the search for truth.

4. Try to discern God's purpose in any of his actions. We always will fall short of doing this, but it is a good starting point when doing theology. Draw from John Wesley's Quadrilateral of Scripture, John asserted that legitimate theological development had to consider Scripture, Tradition, Reason and Experience. If a conclusion was not consistent with all four factors, the conclusion was not legitimate.

DR. RICHARD CHEATHAM

One factor in the present understandings acquired by experts who define the composition of the universe. Frankly, I believe the proper pre-seminary education for potential clergy should include overview course in quantum physics, astronomy, geology, archeology, and world history. You simply cannot speak authoritatively about the will and nature of our Creator unless you have some clear idea of the Creation. Far too much theology is based upon a primitive view of the universe. This makes the conclusions unreasonable.

Another understanding I employ in doing theology is what Paul Tillich believed the essential content lies in the form of the rule or tradition: *Conventionalist* vs. *Traditionalist*. A *Conventionalist* believes that the essence of a rule or tradition resides in the form. If one changes the form in any way they change the essential content. A *Traditionalist* believes that an essential principle pre-existed the form. The form was determined by the culture. Therefore, if anyone attempts to move a rule or tradition to another culture without regard for the new culture's values and traditions, it is akin to trying to convey a liquid in a sieve. The form may arrive intact, but it will have lost its content.

I believe that Jesus stood squarely in the position of a Traditionalist. His Sermon on the Mount clearly displays that. "*You have heard it said, but I say to you.*" Then he expresses an idea that appears to be contradictory to the established rules and values in the culture. He then explains that he did not come to abolish the Law but to fulfill it. In doing so, he digs beneath the surface form to understand and redefine the underlying principle. The Pharisees of his time did not understand this, so they opposed what he did.

History is a rather late development of human culture. Long before there was a concern for recording past events, there were stories that spoke of larger, universal realities. As a young boy, I was fascinated with the Norse, Greek and Roman mythologies. I was too young to understand their depth, but their tales resonated with me. Carl Jung, in his pursuit of dream interpretation as a tool for psychoanalysis, became aware that many of his patients experienced dreams that were strongly reminiscent of some of the ancient mythologies—even though his patients were unaware of those tales. He came to believe that those dreams were messages from the deeper genuine Self we might call the soul, but he called "*The imago Dei.*" They represent understandings of what is occurring deep within the individual.

Every culture has its creation myths. They tell of the culture's understanding of itself and its purpose. The Jewish Scriptures tell two quite different stories. Editing has placed them in juxtaposition, but they were written many centuries apart. The more primitive myth tells of God fashioning a male human from clay, creating a female companion for him from one of his ribs, then placing them in a garden. He orders them not to eat of the tree with the fruit of knowledge, but they disobey him. The consequence is that they are exiled from the garden and forced to labor in order to survive (Genesis 2).

The development of scholarly biblical criticism has provided the tools for being able to ascertain the time and probable location of original writings. Since a living language evolves, those schooled in ancient languages can easily discern the time of origin. A quick example would be that if you watched an older movie and the term "swell" was used to indicate pleasant, you can be sure the movie was made in the 40's. Therefore, we know the later Creation myth was written during the era of the Babylonian Exile in the 6th century BCE. (Genesis 1) The understanding of the universe had expanded, due to the development of astrology by the Babylonians. They had developed a seven-day week, in which the days were named for the planets, in what was believed to be a descending order. The largest celestial object was the Sun (and therefore was considered to be the closest). Therefore, the first day of the week was named "Sunday." Moonday was the next. Saturn was the seventh, and was considered to be an unlucky sign. Therefore, no projects were begun on Saturday.

The exiled Jewish community wanted to affirm the essential goodness of Creation, and the myth took that form. Male and female were created equally and at the same time, and were said to be in God's image. There was no Garden of Eden and work was not a punishment. Rather, humanity was given dominion over the earth in all its goodness. Unfortunately, the two tales were placed in juxtaposition, and many careless readers simply do not notice that they are two distinctly different tales. A simple definition of a myth is that it is a tale that may not be true on the outside, but is saying something quite profound on the inside. In his monumental work, *The Hero with a Thousand Faces,* Joseph Campbell writes, "*It has always been the function of mythology and rite to supply the symbols that carry the human spirit forward, in contradiction to those constant human fantasies that tend to tie it back.*" (p.7) The Book of Genesis is rich with myths. Also, the parables of Jesus are what I call *mini-myths.* Again, citing Campbell: "*It would not be too much to say that myth is the secret opening through which the inexhaustible energies of the cosmos pour into the human cultural manifestation.*" (p.1)

Jesus told stories that penetrated the veneer of superficialities and touched the soul. Those who heard him were and pondered his words were changed— at least in the way in which they would think. If they were hungry enough they would continue to chew on his words and digest them into the depth of their being. They would— in the finest sense repent— a simple term that called for the transformation of the mind. Upon doing so, their allegiance would be transferred from the physical things of earth to the spiritual realities of God. Unfortunately, most who hear or read those words are akin to the seeds that fell on bad soil and are lost. Spiritual dynamism is displaced by religious practice.

Introduction

As a nation, we have lost our soul. The essential problem with American Christianity is that far too many of us have allowed religious beliefs to displace spiritual realities. There is no other explanation for what has occurred and is occurring in our culture. We have become less civil to one another. Violence is epidemic in our nation. Although there are many charitable individuals giving freely of themselves, there seems to be an increasing number of "Me First" people who ignore basic rules of conservation and ecology. The disparity between the "Haves" and "Have-nots" is widening. Selfishness and greed abound. There is a serious disconnect between our physical and spiritual natures.

A sense of loneliness and/or emptiness prevails in far too many people. It has been estimated that the overwhelming majority of people are dissatisfied with their jobs or professions. Illegal drugs are a major social problem, as people seek to either bring some relief, excitement— or pure escape into their seemingly meaningless lives. Southern Poverty Law claims there are nearly 900 hate groups operating and even recruiting in our nation.

Beginning with Constantine in the 4th century AD, the Christian faith- as a whole— has been more of a political instrument than a means for service and spiritual growth. Constantine knew the gods of Rome had lost their power (few believed in them). He saw Christianity as a tool for uniting the empire. However, he soon realized there was a dramatic split with this newly-forming religion. Many believe that Jesus was *identical* with God, while others believed he was *similar*. He pushed to resolve the difference and in the Council of Nicea in 325 A.D., Jesus was declared identical with God, even though this was not supported by Scripture.

The Crusades were poorly manufactured opportunities to raid other communities and expand influence. The leaders feared the influence of Islam, and this was an opportunity to reduce that influence. The cathedral at Cologne, Germany was built to house the remnants of the three magi, that were stolen from a Christian church in a raid by a crusading team.

The medieval church— with its corruption, is a blight on our history. Wealthy nobility purchased Episcopal offices for their younger male heirs. This insured them of being able to live at the level of nobility. Many of these, including a few popes, were more interested in governing and self-indulgences than in the spiritual well-being of their subjects.

The Reformation was supported by German nobility who wished to rid their nation of a foreign leader selected by the pope. Luther served as a great rallying point for them. Luther, incidentally, was more aligned with the nobility than with the common people. He wrote a letter to the German nobility calling upon them to "*strike, smite and slay*" the peasants in their rebellion. He assured them that if they died in the process their souls would immediately be received in Heaven.

Our own rationale of religious superiority for stealing the land from the Native Americans— was an example of this heresy. Except for a few within the religious community, there was no concern for saving souls— only for seizing the land.

The disconnect between soul and ego has been going on for centuries. It is time to address it.

Your Ego

The Greek term *ego* is the first person singular or "*I.*" Our ego is our conscious self. It is that strong sense of self that guides our everyday thoughts and activities. A strong, healthy ego is the foundation for success in life. A strong ego is not to be confused with a large ego. A large ego is one that has weak boundaries and reaches beyond where it properly belongs. It intrudes on others. A strong, healthy ego is keenly aware of what it believes and values. It is not easily swayed, and feels no need "to go along to get along." A strong ego knows its boundaries, but is not so much "other-directed" as "inner directed". Experts claim that our ego begins to develop at about half way through our second year. We become more fully aware of ourselves and sense our separation from others. We develop boundaries. Parents call this era "The Terrible Two's." The words "Me," "Mine," "No," are used frequently by the young developing ego. Soothing words and comfortable hugging no longer have the desired effect. This introduces a new critical period in the child's soul development. The child will try every possible way to get her or his own way. Where the child governed by the soul sought peace, security and comfort, the new ego-driven child is responding to the values and rhythms of the newly-discovered world. Egos want to possess whatever attracts them. What they want, they want immediately, and they will do what is necessary to get it— immediately. We all have seen this acted out by children in restaurants or malls. The parents are embarrassed and often overreact.

DR. RICHARD CHEATHAM

It is our ego that guides our physical, social life. It determines what we shall wear and eat, how we shall earn a living— and all the many other details that shape our life. Through most of our early lives, it is the self— or ego— that generates thought. The embodied ego is drawn to the values of the society in which it lives. It seeks success in all its earthly forms: money power, popularity, security, pleasure— all the attributes that mark a person as successful. There is a ladder to climb and all our energies are focused upon scaling that to as high as we can.

Major life patterns develop as the ego matures. A basic value system emerges. It will be in contrast to the value system of the soul, and this will be a constant life struggle. It is the daily struggle Paul mentions in Romans 9:17, "*The good that I would do is not what I do, but the evil I would not do is what I do.*" It is the ongoing struggle that Jesus alludes to when he tells his followers to seek the treasures of heaven rather than the treasures of earth (Matthew 6:19-21). Carl Jung compared the mind of the ego as the logos- or rational— part of our being. It immediately grasps the ideas presented, and if the mind likes the idea it will try to convince the will to accept the idea, as well. The will, however, is driven by rather primitive forces and does not respond well to the suggestions of the mind. This is a part of Paul's dilemma. Carl Jung claims the soul is the agricultural portion of our being. It heals and grows slowly. I draw from that understanding to interpret the parables of Jesus.

When I studied at the Jungian Institute in Zurich, Switzerland, I learned that Carl Jung differentiated between the ego and the soul by calling the ego the self (lower case s) and the soul the Self (capital S) or *Imago Dei (Image of God)*.

The self (ego), as it develops, often is contacted by the Self (soul) that tries to serve as a guide. This attempt might be missed or ignored. The manner in which the parents handle these incidents develop some life patterns that may— or may not— be healthy. If bullying works that pattern might emerge. If politeness and restraint work, that pattern might emerge. A strong ego is a necessity for good parenting. I am not suggesting harshness. Rather, firmness is the requirement. The parent is experienced. The child is not. The parent needs to be respected— more than liked. Both, of course, is the ideal. However, too many children have been raised by parents who did not want to anger their child, so they acquiesce, and condone disobedience. More often, they are raised by parents who either do not know how to be a proper parent, or do not want to give the time and energy essential to good parenting. The developing ego may recognize that anger can be used as a tool and adopts it as a methodology for attaining what is desired. I found that firmness with fairness made the proper combination for me as a parent. If I set a rule and one of my daughters thought it unfair, I listened to their arguments. There was a clear understanding, however, that any display of anger would immediately end the discussion and my rule would remain intact. If the opposition was rational and there was no danger involved, I often altered the rule. This, frankly, was to help my daughters acquire negotiating skills. If their negotiations never were successful, they would eventually acquiesce and become compliant. Parents would do well to decide and agree upon the behavior patterns they wish to foster.

In speaking of the tension between Self and self at this stage, I find Jesus' parable of the sown seeds to be useful. He speaks of the seeds sown on a hardened path, on loose, rocky soil, or on tares, and on good, fertile soil. The hardened path is the typical young, eager ego. It is responding to the many demands essential for earthly success. Any concern for the soul is lost in the hustle and bustle of everyday life. We see that regularly. As a pastor, I encountered that with painful regularity. Church, for most young couples, was something you attended when you had a free Sunday. The pressures of our society at the time caused one to believe that "good people attend church." Since they wished to think of themselves as good people, they attended church.

And they were "good people." They supported the schools, volunteered for community service jobs, got along well with their neighbors, and essentially obeyed the laws. They enjoyed the fellowship, and often felt they had gained something of value from the worship. They usually left the building feeling uplifted and refreshed. Their life, however, tended to be governed by "shoulds" and "oughts." The ego understood what was required, but had to be guided by an act of the will. None of the potential value of their faith reached to their souls. Their conversations tended to be ego-driven and usually were a mixture of what I call "chit chat." When they discussed religion, the discussion usually centered on items from Scripture. In fact, one's awareness and ability to cite Scripture were considered elements of success. Most adult Sunday school classes were totally focused upon Scripture. They were not designed to facilitate speaking of personal issues.

I recall a young man who told me he would not be as active in the church as he had been. The reason was that his employers had given him a positive evaluation, and told him if he worked harder he would earn a promotion. He dropped out of the extra activities at the church and committed himself to becoming successful. Another young couple moved to a nicer neighborhood. They had shown great promise at spiritual growth. I had begun to think of them as one of my successes, and was delighted for them. They believed the extra time it required to continue with the church was wasteful, and transferred to a small, more conservative church, where their budding growth leveled out. I encountered them years later and noted they were happy and somewhat active in their church... but our conversation was at the level of chit chat. Both cases were instances where the ego decided to ignore the urging of the soul. The surface demands of the ego for these and many,

many others, were too powerful to resist, and the seeds were gobbled up in the rush up the ladder.

During my active ministry, I encountered this type of situation far too many times. Good people allowed themselves to become sidetracked. I could write pages about those excursions, but suffice it to say, most of the people were good, honest, hard-working people who allowed themselves to be caught up in the value system of their egos.

I was caught up in the second issue— the rocky soil. I later observed it far too many times. I had attended church while growing through childhood, but it actually meant nothing to me. I found the sermons and classes boring and unrelated to my life in any way. When I married, however, I attended regularly with my bride. I had attended regularly during our courtship and it seemed irresponsible of me to quit. I still found it boring, however. Then, at Ft. Sill while preparing to go to Korea as an artillery officer, we attended a church in which the preacher made God and Jesus relevant for me. I sprung up like the seed in soft soil. I was totally committed to my new-found faith. However, the chaplain in Korea was filled with "shoulds" and "oughts," and very negative. Added to that was the degradation and destruction I witnessed, and I returned home as a functional atheist, unable to believe in a loving deity who would allow that.

Needless to say, I worked my way beyond that. However, I have seen far too many who gave up on their faith because of their immature understanding of the faith. When it did not work as they wished, they had no roots to sustain them.

I view the seeds sown in the tares as the Word planted in those who have filled their inner selves with too many bad values. They have allowed themselves to become slaves to some form of vice— physical or mental. Some have developed patterns of dishonesty that obscure the values of the soul. Broadly speaking, for me, these tares represent the addictive personalities whose obsessions choke out the essential message for the soul.

A strong ego is absolutely essential for genuine spiritual growth. Jesus cautioned about those who start the process, but quit along the way. Quitting probably was the result of a weak ego. Those with weak ego for example, tend to adjust their personalities to the group. They behave differently in different groups. This is the reason that many solid, respectable people misbehave when they are in a more reckless group. They adjust in order to be accepted— to "fit in." Many a marriage counselor has encountered the situation where one partner says they will be whatever their partner wants, in order to maintain the security of the relationship. That in itself is usually a key to the problem the couple faces. Two strong egos will clash, but work out their differences if both have good values. However, when you try to pair a strong ego with a weak ego you are heading for some kind of difficulty. One will dominate— and yet be unhappy that they do not encounter a stronger personality to embrace and work with.

Far too many people have jobs or professions that are not of their choosing. Often, they were to fulfill the expectation or desire of another person (usually a parent). They may earn a good financial living, but find little joy or satisfaction in what they do. Many people either make or dream of making a dramatic change in their profession during their 30's. They either have tired of their role or awakened to a greater calling within themselves. One interesting example of this was a school friend who was quite independent in everything he did, but also exceptionally intelligent. At college he became a conformist, of sorts, class president of his sophomore, junior and senior class. He was offered a high-paying job as an engineer that included time and expenses to earn a masters' degree. I saw him in his late 20's and all seemed well. Then one day I encountered him and he was wearing a plaid woolen shirt as he had in high school days. He also was sporting a five-o'clock shadow. "What happened?" I asked. "Got tired of sitting at a desk. I'm now a tree surgeon."

An even more dramatic event involved a woman who had followed the family pattern of becoming a bank teller. It was expected of her. Everyone from the grandfather down to her had been a bank teller. It was an honest, decent profession. The pay was not great, but was steady and dependable. She married a rather staid gentleman and settled into and quiet, orderly life. In her 30's however, she began to feel a deep sense of dissatisfaction— not only with what she was doing— but for who she was. She felt artificial— unreal— and hungered to follow that urge to wherever it led her. As part of her search, she took a Myers-Briggs personality test that revealed her to be quite different from her family members. She went into counseling and began to feel a deeply-seated difference in herself. During this time, her husband complained about the changes, and finally told her to stop the counseling or he would divorce her. She continued— they divorced. She emerged as an awakened, vital personality and found a new profession dealing extensively with people at a personal level.

What I appreciated and wondered at during my reading of her story was the change that obvious had taken place in her ego that allowed— forced— her to make the difficult journey to newness and wholeness. She obviously had been compliant when younger and selecting a career path. She did what others wanted and expected. Somewhere along the line, however, her ego (genuine sense of self) became strong and bold enough to abandon the relationships and become authentic. I am reminded of Jesus admonition that those who were not willing to hate (his words) his/her family in order to become part of God's Kingdom, were unworthy of the Kingdom.

DR. RICHARD CHEATHAM

If anyone comes to me and does not hate his father, mother, wife and children, brother and sister, and— yes— even his own life— he cannot be my disciple. (Luke 14:26)

This was an extreme case, but we all have observed the family scapegoat who wants to improve his life, but is held back by the family— that has a need for a scapegoat. The enabling spouse who supports the drinking, gambling or whatever addiction is crippling and spiritually imprisoning the family member. Jesus words are extreme, but he often employed hyperbole to make a point. A person with a weak ego will remain a functional non-disciple as far as spiritual development is concerned.

How did this woman gain the strength to break free? Somewhere in the answer is a clue for how anyone of us can strengthen our ego to become self-sufficient and self-confident enough to guide our own development as children of God.

I believe it is possible to strengthen our egos by disciplined effort. Our ego is part of our humanity. As part of the process of strengthening our egos we must draw from our deeper self— our soul. I believe our soul has a steady focus upon things spiritual. It also is incessantly trying to communicate with our ego— to give it advice and direction. One way in which it appears to do this is to generate a sense of dissatisfaction within us when we are not on the proper path. Following a path of psychological development from Carl Jung, I find that there are a couple of critical ages when this is most apt to occur: age 30 and age 42 (give or take a few years for either). In her book, *Passages*, Gail Sheehy wrote of Catch 30 when she believed the first critical period appeared. By that time, we have fulfilled the expectations of society insofar as education, career and marriage are involved. We find ourselves singing the old Peggy Lee song, "Is That All There Is?" I vividly recall, at that age, having completed my task of lawn mowing. I was doing well financially in the family boat business, I had a nice starter home, a new car, a lovely wife and two adorable daughters. I was well on my way to a successful life. However, I recall surveying my handiwork and asking myself, "*Is this what my life is to be about: a nicer house, and more expensive car, a club membership somewhere, selling big-boy toys and properly maintaining my yard so the neighbors will think well of me?*" Within a year, I received a powerful call to enter the Christian ministry, and began to live a life that has been infinitely more rewarding than the one I had been working to create.

Rollo May used a term, *ontological anxiety* to express this dynamic. He said that we feel some underlying pressure to become something that gives meaning to our lives. We unconsciously search for that which gives specific values of personality. In most cases, we have no idea what that might be. It is this vague awareness that we must become more than we are— something that causes us to feel our lives have meaning. The irony is that we tend to try to dismiss this feeling of emptiness by a variety of false and wasteful means. "When the going gets tough, the tough go shopping," is a common escape avenue. The malls overflow with people shopping for things they really do not need. The purchase creates a temporary release from anxiety, but soon returns. As a consequence, yard sales, garage sales and rummage sales abound in our society ... and few recognize the waste— of time— of money and of raw resources better saved for future generations. Our waste landfills also overflow.

Addictive behavior is becoming increasingly widespread. The ultimate goal of every addiction is to avoid intimacy— with others and one's self. We are aware of the effects of drugs and alcohol addictions. They dissolve relationships and cause the addicts to become emotional cripples. However, there are many other forms of addiction that are less obvious, but equally destructive. They are forms of what is called "busyness addiction." By immersing ourselves in activities we avoid any reflection on our own lives. As a practical matter, any activity can become an instrument for addiction. Television, internet, computer games, and cellphones are painfully obvious. We all have observed couples who are engaged in a cellphone conversation with someone not present. We also have observed young people totally absorbed in a meaningless computer game. Most activities can be useful and means for enhancing the quality of life, but they also can become the tools of addiction. If they take precedence over relationships or even your own need for times of quiet reflection, they can become destructive.

An insidious form of busyness addiction is what I call "noise addiction." Most people driving alone play their radios. They listen to the news or enjoy some music. It is harmless. It also is not helpful— for spiritual development. Carl Jung told of a patient who was successful as a lawyer and had all the accouterments of a good life by cultural standards. However, he suffered a generalized anxiety. Jung suggested the man take a day each week to be by himself. After two weeks, the man returned to Jung and reported he felt no better. Jung inquired as to how the man had spent his quiet day. The first week he had played his collection of Beethoven and read Shakespeare's sonnets. The second week he had listened to his Mozart and read Tennyson. Jung responded angrily, "I told you to spend the day with yourself— not Beethoven, Shakespeare, Mozart and Tennyson!" The man was taken aback and replied: "Just by myself? That would drive me crazy!" "This," responded Jung, "is the self you impose on others for ten to fourteen hours a day?" The man understood. He began to spend his quiet days in quiet reflection, and the healing began.

I strongly recommend that the serious spiritual pilgrim spend some time in honest self-appraisal. This can be accomplished, in part, by quiet meditation, and— again, in part— within a small group. Within the group, you can develop the trust and self-confidence to voice your honest views on all aspects of your life. Share what you believe are your strengths— and your weaknesses. Share your views on values and be able to explain your reasons. The group should have at least three people and no more than five. Tell your story, and support the others as they tell theirs and share their values and views. I believe you will find the inner confidence growing until you truly have an ego strong enough to give you greater autonomy.

This process of stillness and reflective meditation requires time and patience. Many of us feel uncomfortable with absolute silence What you seek will not occur for months— perhaps years. Your life movement should be from the egocentricity that began shortly after your birth, to Theocentricity— centered in your soul, and in communion with God. The Kingdom of God is not some future possibility. Jesus' message at the start of his ministry was, "*The Kingdom of God is at hand. Repent and believe the good news." (Mark 1:15)*. The Greek word we translate as repent (*metanoia*) actually means to transform the mind— after careful consideration. In his letter to the Romans (12:2), Paul writes, "*Do not be conformed to the world, but be transformed by the renewing of your mind.*" In secular terms, Paul was telling his readers to stop living only out of their egos, and to be in touch with the deeper, truer part of who they were. This called for a disciplined mind and commitment. Unfortunately, the term, *repent,* became terribly distorted over the years, and causes so many of us to miss the point. We hear it in terms of wallowing in remorse, guilt and confession of sins. Unfortunately, our Christian faith lost its way, from liberating, guiding and empowering worthy and fulfilling lives, to controlling, limiting and generally degrading what it means to be human. I want to begin our focus upon what I call the soul. It is our soul— our healthy soul— that can lift us from who we are to who God intends for us to be.

I stated that major life patterns develop as the ego matures, and a basic value system emerges. It will be in contrast to the value system of the soul, and this will be a constant life struggle. It is that daily struggle Paul mentioned in Romans 9:17, about not being able to do the good, but doing the evil. It is the ongoing struggle that Jesus alludes to when he tells his followers to seek the treasures of heaven rather than the treasures of earth (Matthew 6:19-21).

Your Soul ... and Mine

In dealing with the ego, I have made some mention of the function of the soul. At this point I want to focus fully upon this portion of ourselves we call *the soul*. Our spiritual dimension resides deeply within our inner being, buried in the unconscious. I do not believe one can locate specifically where the soul is located. Rather, I think of it as the spiritual body that is an underlying part of who we are. In 1 Corinthians 15:44, Paul writes of our body in this way: "*It is sown a natural body, it is raised a spiritual body.*" It is that eternal dimension of our being It resides everywhere within us— as much in our toes as in our brain. Yet, it cannot be discerned by any known means. As I have pointed out, where the ego is concerned with life in the physical world, the soul is focused upon the spiritual realm. When discussing any subject, I find it useful to clarify key definitions. In that way, we all share some mutual understanding of the topic. The term *soul* is so broadly used as to have a nebulous meaning at best. I will share my understanding, and even though you may not totally agree, at least you will have some idea of what I am trying to express. I draw a bit from the ancients as a starting point. I believe the soul is the essential nature of our being. It is the eternal portion that is most in contact with what we call "The Divine." When manifested in our personality it is what we call "character." A healthy soul produces a person of strong and good character. We view these people as trustworthy, with good judgment. They are respected for their integrity.

DR. RICHARD CHEATHAM

The ancient Greeks believed that the interior of a person contained both a psyche (soul) and a nous (mind). Their interaction was not clear, but it was evident that the soul took precedence over the mind. I have struggled for years to understand how and why a thought emerges into our consciousness. I believe some are just randomly generated by the brain's activity. We are inundated by stimuli that set thoughts in motion. I hear a song from my past and am transported back to an era when that song was popular. We tend to think of that as nostalgia. Memories trigger thoughts rather easily. Dialogue produces thoughts related to the subject at hand.

Still, there are those moments when a totally original thought emerges— or when we seem to hear a quiet voice that offers guidance. Those are the times I believe that our soul is reaching to the ego to give advice and understanding. We all have heard that quiet voice that seems to be drawing from an unknown source of wisdom.

The prophets of the Books of the Old Testament were in tune with their souls. The correct term for them, incidentally is "Prophet of God." A prophet is not one who predicts the future, but one who speaks for God. The term *pro-phete* simply meant "to speak for." As a matter of course, they could look down the road of time and see the inevitable conclusions of our actions, but their calling was as spokespersons for God. We have prophetic voices today, but as with the prophets of olden days, they are not heeded or appreciated, expect in retrospect. It is my experience that many of our prophets are the artists. The same dynamic that allows them to speak for God seems also to inspire them to new, creative ideas.

I noted earlier that the parables Jesus told actually were mini-myths that could not be properly understood by the rational part of our mind. They had to be grasped by our intuition. The dialogue John relates between Jesus and Nicodemus was a clear example of a rational mind trying to grasp what an intuitive mind was saying. (John 3:1-21) One must be able to read the Greek in order to understand and appreciate what was recorded. John uses the term *anathon* in an intentionally ambiguous way to make his point. The more common meaning of the term is *again*. Another meaning is *from above*— which suggests the spiritual realm. Jesus tells Nicodemus that we must be born *anathon* in order to achieve the Kingdom. Nicodemus takes this to mean the person must literally be born a second time. He follows that track, while Jesus is trying to explain a spiritual birth. Nicodemus leaves in confusion— as I believe so many Christian pilgrims live in a confused state because they simply cannot or will not interpret the mythological statements properly.

This Self, that I identify as soul, also speaks to us through our intuition. There have been times when I have caught myself saying something from my intuition that I had to ponder on in order to more fully understand what I meant. My youthful plans for a career was as a jazz musician. I toyed with the academics because I believed I did not need what they offered. At age eighteen I was offered a great opportunity to play with a newly-formed group. The salary was unexpectedly high, and the setting was good. However, I was surprised to hear myself turning the offer down. When asked why, this eighteen year old boy replied, "Because when I am forty-five years old I do not want to be playing in a smoke-filled room for a bunch of drunks." As I reflected on my words I realized that even though I thoroughly enjoyed playing jazz, I did not want the life of a jazz musician. There have been other occasions when some intuitive thought or utterance arose and caused me to evaluate my life goals.

Years later, when I was in the ministry, one of my young daughters who loved to dance was asked to dance at a gathering. She sprang to the floor, but— before she began to move— she seemed to become aware of all the people watching her. In that moment, she shriveled up, crossed her arms over her body as if to cover her nakedness, and slinked off the floor and into a remote corner. I turned to a friend and said, "We have just witnessed the Fall, and it may take her years to be as free as she was a moment ago." In reflecting upon those words, I realized I had put my finger on the source of the biblical myth. We all experience that moment of self-realization when we sense our separation. Our conscious self may forget, but our unconscious recalls and responds to that myth of Fall.

The list is large, but perhaps you get the idea, and perhaps you have had similar moments of rare insight. It is in such moments that I believe our soul is offering advice and understanding. If we listen and heed, life goes well. We move along— a bit more wisely into our future. If we ignore or dismiss it, we miss an opportunity that would have made life fuller.

I know far too many individuals who made their professional decisions based upon either outside pressures or the need for security. They always seem to be looking back over their shoulders as though they lost something. I fervently wish our school system or family system would help a person understand his or her more natural calling, one that would satisfy the soul. *As Jesus asked, "What does it profit a person to gain the world but lose his soul?"* (Mark 8:36) is an appropriate question for young people to be asked.

There was a time when I considered going into law. Then I took stock of myself and admitted I enjoy winning too much for that to be the proper career path for me. I believe I would have become someone I do not want to become. I know my strengths, but I also know my weaknesses. I could skirt the edges of the law in order to achieve an unwarranted victory. I believe it is my inner self— my soul— who guides that understanding. It certainly is not my ego— that enjoys triumphs of any kind. Incidentally, I have become quite aware of the fact that the more I am in touch with my soul or inner Self, the less need I have to win at anything; and the more I enjoy seeing the triumph in my opponents' eyes ... and (quietly) share in their victory.

IN SEARCH OF YOUR SOUL

The Greeks believed there were nine goddesses who watched over the arts and sciences. They would inspire the creative mind to put forth hitherto unimaginable works of beauty and profundity. They were called muses. They inspired their subjects to produce what they otherwise could not have conceptualized. In time, the term muse began to take on the connotation of reflective thought. People muse about a subject. Also, there are artists who consider other people as their muse— their inspiration. That still does not explain how the creative idea actual formulates, however. Something has to spur the original thought, or the moment of "inspiration" will prove fruitless.

The soul contains archetypes that represent every human characteristic. For clarification, they are given names that broadly represent their characteristics. However, the names are not to suggest that the individuals will find some form of employment directly related to those titles. Many of these archetypes will emerge at certain times on our development. Sometimes a situation will call them forth. Sometimes it merely is the proper moment for them to make their entrance. Some archetypes may become dominant, while others may either never appear or will be only subtly apparent. It is the nature of The Self to seek to manifest and develop as many of these archetypal qualities as possible. However, some archetypal development may be hindered, misdirected or essentially dismissed in the process of maturing to adulthood. The goal of the embodied soul is to become complete (the Greek term we translate as *perfect*, is more properly translated as *complete*). My study of Jungian archetypes convinces me that there are far too many facets of personality lying undeveloped, under-developed, and misdirected— residing within me to be properly developed in one or even a hundred lifetimes. An archetype is a quality of personality that has its own energy, script and boundaries.

Normally, our archetypes are fully integrated into our total personality. We are unaware of the emergence and transitions of one to another because it is a natural part of who we are in our complexity. For example, a small group may be having a serious discussion, when someone makes a grammatical error that could be interpreted as a pun. One of the group picks up on it and amplifies with another pun. The mood changes and the once-serious discussion becomes a light-hearted competition to top one another. After a brief time of this, one of the group says, "I think we strayed from our purpose. "A few resettle into a serious dimension but one or two would like to continue with the humor. They may make a stab at doing so, but quickly conform to the will of the group. Shortly back into the subject an issue arises that prompts one of the group to share a health concern. The same ones who had been laughing and joking a moment before suddenly become care givers, expressing genuine concern for the person. The dominant archetype had changed from sage to joker to care-giver in less than five minutes, and was quite natural and normal. However, one of the group may have an undeveloped joker and sat silently during the time of humor. He may have been the person calling the group back to the serious subject. There also might be one with an undeveloped care-giver, who would have been quiet during that episode.

Some of these archetypes are quite common, and I shall name a few as examples:

The Caregiver. This tends to be more common in females than in males. It may manifest itself as playing nurse or mothering dolls. Someone with a dominant Caregiver may find employment in the healing profession. However, they may as easily become clergy, teachers, counselors, homemakers, social workers, or any of a dozen professions where they can provide care for others.

The Warrior is assertive and more self-sufficient. The Warrior enjoys playing war games and is eager for competition. However, most warriors do not end up in the military. They may be salespersons, lawyers, professional athletes, or any number of professions that thrive with competition.

The Scientist is curious and finds ways to satisfy that curiosity. The Scientist may want the chemistry set, or is temporarily satisfied, with dismantling items to see how they work.

The Teacher will enjoy playing school, and may either do so with dolls or with other children. Later, they may work in the area of human resources. They also may find employment that has nothing to do with guiding others, but will find satisfaction as volunteer tutors, Sunday school teachers, Scout leaders or merely mentoring.

The Jester enjoys life and generates humor. A well-developed Jester allows a satisfying play ethic. Jesters can be found anywhere and everywhere. As a rule they enjoy life, however, they also might use humor to compensate for some perceived inadequacy.

The Sage normally appears later in life. It is the bearer of wisdom, and it requires time for wisdom to develop. Only life experiences can accomplish that. Often the Sage will announce its presence in a dream. Some mentor/teacher from the past appears to let you know your Sage is available to you. If a person lives well, the sage will naturally appear in mid or later life, adding wisdom to situations.

The list is endless, and ultimately contains all aspects of human personality. However, the more complete and fully developed your archetypes are, the more fully you will participate in the totality of life

The soul has little concern for physical or cultural matters. These are simply ways of paying the bills and maintaining a somewhat normal life. The soul is primarily concerned with what we call *spiritual matters.* When Jesus admonished his followers not to be concerned with what they would eat or wear, he was addressing their souls. "*Store up treasures in heaven— not on earth,"* (Mathew 6:19-20) was just another way of his trying to make people connect with their divine nature. These spiritual treasures are the abstract qualities of human existence. A few, most-obvious examples are love, generosity, compassion, empathy, and friendliness. Some of these will often conflict with the individual's earthly goals. Too much compassion suggests weakness to some. A person has to have a tough shell to survive and succeed, is a common belief. Generosity interferes with accumulating wealth. You simply cannot keep what you give away. Most of us (even those with a more generous spirit) find ways of justifying the withholding or limiting our charitable gifts.

Throughout our lives our souls will be in dialogue with our egos, determining our spiritual path. The dialogue may take many forms: debate is common. Often it feels like a struggle between the heart and the mind. My Myers/Briggs indicator dubs me as a "Thinker," and I have learned to trust my head over my heart. Others will find the opposite is true for them. One part of you will say "yes," while the other cautions a "no." Robert Frosts' poem, "The Road Not Taken," plays itself constantly in my mind when I find these two essential parts of myself in conversation. The final lines of the poem, occasionally haunt me:

"I shall be telling this with a sigh,
ages and ages hence: two roads diverged in a wood,
and I— I took the one less traveled by,
and that has made all the difference."

Many were the times I made significant decisions, never realizing I was choosing between values of the ego and values of the soul. I just realized one decision seemed of greater long-term value than the other. Unfortunately, I must admit, I did not always choose wisely. There were times when I temporarily lost my way, and damaged some relationships, and learned hard lessons. This is the most common method by which we grow— learning from our mistakes and failures.

We do those things— you and I. We do not always make good choices. That is when this dynamic we call Grace" enters into the picture. I am a great believer in the message of Roman 8:28: *"We know that in all things God works for the good with those who love him and are called according to his purpose."* I have developed various models of how this works, but I really am only speculating in this regard. What I do know is that there is some unseen dynamic that seems to guide and empower me— and others— toward a decent resolution of the issues we face. Pay attention to what is happening. Be as realistic as possible, and adjust to a changing situation. Things get better.

So, these are examples of my understanding of what is meant by soul. I see it as either the interior residue (God within us) or the entrance way to the divine. I see the soul as always looking beyond this life to eternity and doing its best to shape the life to be fully prepared for that experience. I see the soul as the essence of who we are— the quality we call character. When our soul loses its connection with our conscious ego, we are set adrift. We respond to the stimuli of the society— its values and its goals. We become or remain egocentric creatures, far more concerned for ourselves than others. Eventually, we stagnate and our spiritual growth halts. Our circle of concern follows the path of relationships. Our sense of empathy is diminished. We do not understand John Donne's *"Any man's death diminishes me, for I am involved in mankind."* Life takes on a veneer of superficiality, and we spend a great deal of our time in diversions— passing the time— filling the time— rather than using the time.

Attributes of a Healthy Soul

A healthy soul does not allow itself to be defined and shaped by its failures. It recognizes the failures and comes to terms with them. However, it defines itself by its strengths and successes— large and small. Too many people allow their lives to wallow in their sense of inadequacy— rather than to soar with an awareness of their potential to be more than they are.

A tennis coach I knew rarely corrected mistakes. However, on those occasions when I hit a particularly good shot, he stopped and inquired what I did. I was learning what I did that was good, rather than just correcting what did not work. I also had a clarinet instructor who cautioned me to practice only at the speed where I could play every note properly. Once my fingers knew where to go, the speed would pick up. "Do not rehearse your mistakes!" he would say.

It is the task of one's spiritual guide to allow the individual to soar. Jesus said to the strangers on the hill, "*You are the light of the world. Let the light shine!*" (Matthew 5:14). This is the primary reason I abhor the standard prayer of confession that is required prior to receiving communion. It has failure built in. We know when we return we will admit failure. The prayer demands it. We rehearse our failures rather than celebrating our strengths.

There are a series of attributes that a healthy soul contains. For most of us, they begin as acts of the will. With the passage of time, and thoughtful, reflective effort, however, they eventually become attributes of a healthy soul. In no particular order, I will present a few and speak of their development and importance. These qualities all blend together, of course. They interweave to form a healthy soul that reflects the better part of our humanity.

1. Empathy

A healthy soul will feel empathy with others. This is absolutely essential to the foundation or a healthy soul. It senses a presence that has all the longings, struggles, fears, aspirations and joys. Years ago, a popular song declared, "I want to be happy, but I can't be happy, till I make you happy, too." Another declared, "when I saw you crying, I cried, too." A healthy soul senses the feelings of another, and relates appropriately.

Far too many times we act more as an audience than a participant, when someone is sharing an issue important to them. I recall my clinical training at the University of Michigan Hospital. Many times, I entered a patient's room filed with visitors. Far too often they were passing the time, entertaining themselves. They felt some obligation to be present, but they did not want the emotional involvement that accompanied any genuine interest in the patients—or what was happening in their lives. Many who engaged the patients defended themselves by their denial of the seriousness of the illness. They played the positive cards, "You're looking good!" "We can't wait for you to get out of here and back to normal." Even the question, "How are you doing?" can be stated in such a way as to deny the possibility of an honest response.

In all candor, when I did my clinical training, I had times when I was more concerned with protecting myself than caring for the patient. One patient in particular upset me. He was about my age, had two children (as I did, then), he had begun a new job and was beginning to thrive in it (as I had just entered the ministry and was doing well). The problem was that he was dying ... and I was not. A part of me was keenly aware that I could have been the one dying. Another part felt guilt, because I went home every night and he never would. I planned my visits to coincide with doctor's rounds in order to keep them short. I hastened in— and out— with as much dignity as I could muster, and never allowed myself to empathize with the patient. The supervising chaplain helped me to understand what was happening within me, and assured me that he and others were picking up the pieces. It was a terrible, eye-opening— and humiliating experience for me, but I learned the lesson. We simply cannot relate meaningfully to others unless we are willing to risk emotional pain.

Unless we are open to suffer with the other person, we really cannot fully rejoice with them when some victory is attained. It is the difference between being a spectator and a participant. The fan in the stands never can experience the same sense of elation as the participants on the field. Unfortunately, there is no simple way to attain this. Empathy for some, is as natural as breathing. Most of us, however, have a natural defense that makes it more difficult. During clinical training, we were required to make a verbatim of difficult encounters. Within the confines of a small group we shared the verbatim and responded to the comments and questions of the group members. The most common question was, "You changed the subject. Why?" I never realized how I used this simple device to protect myself from difficult situations or painful emotions. It was a natural part of who I had become. Sometimes our egocentricity gets in the way. We become more concerned with telling our story than in listening and understanding the other person. As a result, we become mere conversationalists and not counselors or supporters.

For me, the task of developing empathy— genuine empathy— was one of self-awareness. I monitored my evasive tactics, came to terms with them ... and grew. Near the end of my clinical training I had a parishioner ask me to visit a friend who was dying, but could not talk about it. I knew, trusted and respected the parishioner, so I accepted the offer. The conversation actually ran like this:

"Hello, I'm Dick Cheatham, Ardele's pastor. She asked me to drop by to see you."

"Come in, please."

"How are you doing?"

"Not well."

"What's happening?"

"I'm dying."

"Would you like to talk about that?" and we delved into the subject and spent the next hour or so there.

Somewhere along the line, I had learned to drop all self-concern and focus entirely on the other person. She sensed that and was more-than-ready to talk about the great adventure that lay ahead.

2. Agape

Agape is one of the Greek terms we translate as love. *Eros* denotes a romantic love and *philo* denotes what we call "brotherly love." Actually, the earlier translations of *agape* used the term "charity," not love. The King James version of 1 Corinthians 13:13 says, "faith, hope and charity." Unfortunately, the connotation changed with time, and "charity" began to be thought as a dispassionate dispensing of a gift. The public wanted more, so some translator decided that the term "love" would serve as a replacement. However, the term love, is too vague to denote anything specific. "I love a parade!" "I love traveling." "I love a good steak." More often than not, the term denotes a sense of pleasure when engaged in a desired activity.

A beloved, but poorly translated passage is John 3:16: *"For God so loved the world."* The term translated as "so" actually means "thus" or "in this manner." A correct translation would read, *"For in this manner God loved (agape) the world"*. The term *agape*, in this case obviously calls for action. Without the action, there could be no *agape*.

All this is a way of saying that Christian love *(agape)* is not mere emotion. It must be accompanied by a nurturing action in order to have substance. Also, it has nothing to do with liking— or feeling positive affection. Jesus called for his followers to love *(agape)* their enemies. He did not suggest we like them. Rather, his concern was that we show some care for the well-being of all others— including those who would harm us in some way.

That's tough stuff! Military medics and the Red Cross come the closest to fulfilling that charge. The uniform is not important. The person is. We also see this characteristic in a sport such as football. Opposing players do their best to knock their opponent out of a play. They block hard and tackle hard. Part of their goal in doing so is to dominate the play, but another part is to punish the opponent and make him think before catching a pass or making a tackle. However, when a player is injured and timeout is called, players from both teams line up in concern for the injured one. They did not want to damage the person permanently. Suddenly, they experience *agape* in their concern for the other's well-being.

So where does that leave most of us? How concerned for the well-being of others are we, really? My mail constantly contains legitimate calls for financial assistance for some worthy cause. Most I discard without opening— not because I do not care, but primarily because I have exhausted my charitable resources and do not want to feel worse for not being able to help.

I believe we all have been there. We have a limit as to how much discretionary cash we can distribute to others in need. Every year, we create a charitable budget schedule— and then exceed it. Again, many of you understand that. There always is some new appeal that touches our heart and requires us to write a check. I want us to think in terms apart from financial when we consider the ramifications of Christian love. We have time and we have talents. Sharing these can be of greater significance than a few more dollars thrown in the pool. There are lonely people we know who could use a visit or a phone call ... just to chat. There are an endless number of volunteer positions open at hospitals, nursing homes, schools and service organizations. Most Rotary clubs function more as a community service group than as a private dining club. There are lonely people in the military who would greatly appreciate a box of goodies complete with a letter while serving in some desolate area of the world.

Do you want to grow in Christian love? Then start loving.

3. Acceptance

This is quite different from forgiveness. It is acceptance of who the other person is— as that person is— without negative judgment. In every friendship I have ever made, I recognize the less desirable traits within that friend. I might wish they were not there, but, then I realize I undoubtedly also have some negative traits that my friend has accepted as a part of who I am.

Acceptance is based on the understanding that— as humans— we all have flaws of some sort. Some of these may have been groomed in childhood. Others may simply be indigenous to who we are. Some of us are more intelligent. Some of us may be more courageous. Some are more loving by their nature ... and in every instance, I could have substituted "less" for "more" and still have been accurate. I certainly am not all I wish I were. Why would anyone think I was?

I recall encountering a student at seminary who really bothered me. He was too outspoken— too openly critical of too many people and too many things. I avoided him, even leaving rooms where he held court.

I definitely was not accepting of him. Then I recalled a motto I adopted years ago: "*If you do not like me that is your problem; if I do not like you that is my problem. I cannot help you with yours, but I must work on mine.*" I had to ask myself what it was about him I disliked, and why that bothered me. I braced myself and gave it a try. It was somewhat akin to trying to get near someone who kept flailing away with wild fists. His bombastic style kept us at a distance. He wanted to speak, but not listen. He did not seem interested in developing relationships— just proclaiming— authoritatively— how competent he was by his negativity.

I persisted, and eventually we shared conversations. Once he let his guard down, I saw a somewhat frightened person, trying to preserve a sense of competence in a new and difficult situation. He was quite successful as a sales engineer when he received an irresistible call to become a clergyman. He returned to being a student— after a long hiatus— and was unsure (as we all were) about being able to compete with the younger crowd. He also was beginning a long and difficult process of losing his eyesight. He had a fine quality mind, and was employing it to prop up his own ego that he believed was under siege.

Once I understood who he was, acceptance was a given. We became friends— good friends. I learned much from that experience. We all have private parts of ourselves that shape who we are. When I prowl through the hidden recesses of my own mind, I recognize events and experiences that have given me some of the idiosyncrasies that undoubtedly call for acceptance from friends. Jesus statement to *"judge not, because you are measured by your judgment."* (Matthew 7:1) is so glaringly true that it should give pause to anyone who makes even private negative judgments on others. God— through Christ— calls us to love one another. Judgment is not on our menu ... and should not be ordered.

We simply do not— and cannot— know the burdens that others carry. Our task is to help one another along life's path. Part of that calls for acceptance.

4. Gratitude

An attitude of gratitude can radically change one's perspective on life. We did very little to fashion our life and the world we live in. Essentially, we were somewhat passive recipients of a multitude of graciousness. Parents, teachers, mentors did more to shape us than we imagine. Unknown citizens who constructed the infrastructure and the buildings provided us with a lifestyle we too often take for granted.

I believe any lack of gratitude we have comes from excessive egocentricity. We seem to believe we are entitled to what we deem as desirable. We take the many gifts of life for granted, and concentrate our efforts upon achieving or attaining ... more. We do not begin to focus upon the efforts of others to have made our life-style possible. I see this quite often with children of parents who are financially successful. Even their attitude in a classroom is one of indifference. They seem to believe that the physical quality of life will be maintained with little effort on their part. In contrast, I recall sponsoring two students to an elementary education in Zimbabwe, Africa. One of the letters they sent said, "Please take care of yourselves, because if anything happens to you, I am in trouble." The children who attended that school understood that the opportunity to receive an education was a precious gift. For them, it meant the difference between poverty and a decent living. It also meant the difference of living a life of ignorance or one where increased understanding was possible. They had seen poverty and ignorance and wanted neither. Their essential attitude toward education was one of gratitude. School was an opportunity— an adventure to be relished.

More often, however, what I observe as a lack of gratitude is our overlooking the many miracles that surround us daily. Dawn for many comes as an interruption. I vividly recall some early friends and acquaintances who made me more aware of the wonder of watching darkness turn to light— of a new day being formed as we do nothing but prepare ourselves for that day. Not everyone who went to bed the night before gets to witness this wonder. There will be many who— having no idea— will discover that that they have seen their last dawning. To be called forth into a new day is a gift not everyone receives. Then there are those for whom a new day is but another day that offers a search for survival. We who have refrigerators and pantries that offer an abundance of culinary opportunities are far more fortunate than the majority of those who share this planet with us.

I recall a young man who always applauded the sunset, often crying out "Author! Author!" as he stood, clapping his hands in appreciation for the beauty of the setting sun. The atmosphere softens the light and creates an orange or reddish hue that *bathes the landscape in a color that* (to cite James Whitcomb Riley) *"no painter has the coloring to mock."* The clouds reflect that reddish— even pinkish hue— that creates a mystical sense of beauty that too soon fades.

In my reflective moments, I consider the wonder of God's gracious love in the manner he created us. He has filled the world with beauty, but he also bestowed upon us a sense of beauty. God meant for us to appreciate the beauty he created. It was for us that the beauty exists. We respond well to it. It does a multitude of useful things to us. It can sooth or excite. It can give a sense of pure pleasure. Beauty has the ability to open avenues of the mind, to cause us to ponder issues that are not tangible. More than giving us an appreciation for beauty in sight, sound and smell, God has empowered us humans to create beauty in various forms. If this understanding does not generate some sense of gratitude, then I do not know what will.

An attitude of gratitude is at least gently aware of these simple everyday gifts we take for granted. When I hear a musician of the caliber of Josh Groban, Jackie Evancho or Katherine Jenkins, I lift a silent word of thanksgiving to God for giving the world such talent. The same is true whenever I encounter some artistic talent that makes the world more beautiful. You and I do nothing to deserve such beauty, but God— through His graciousness— continually bestows such beauty upon us. An attitude of gratitude opens our hearts and minds to receive and appreciate the many wonders that come our way— for which we have done nothing to deserve. It turns life into a party of sorts, in which we as guests are showered with gifts from unseen hosts.

5. Generativity

Generativity, as I learned the term at seminary refers to our ability to create for others. Generativity versus stagnation is the seventh of eight stages of Erik Erikson's theory of psychosocial development. Contributing to society and doing things to benefit future generations are important needs at the generativity versus stagnation stage of development.

Erikson pits generativity against its opposite: stagnation. He claims that one or the other dynamic will become central in us with the passage of time. I have observed thousands of elderly people who determine that they will spend their final days in some form or self-entertainment. Those days are spent in what I call pastimes. They play games that ultimately are meaningless. According to Erikson, this eventually deteriorates into stagnation. The participants could echo the words from Ecclesiastes: *"Futility, futility! All is futility, and there is nothing new under the sun."* (12:8) They may tell themselves they are enjoying their retirement, but for practical purposes, they have stopped living productive, meaningful lives. Whatever zest once was present, diminishes. Life becomes a routine.

I find great satisfaction in watching some younger person succeed in a new venture. As a teacher, I sense elation when I see a mind opening with a new understanding— or a product completed by a newly-acquired skill. To be a part of the process generates far more satisfaction than shooting par, holding a straight flush or making a grand slam bid. It is not a matter of believing that some part of myself resides in the initiate. Rather it is the awareness that having done the major work of this earthly life, I have helped a new generation emerge to take our places. We pass life down to ensuing generations. That is God's plan— and that is good enough for me.

This empowerment of younger people may take many forms. It may be in the form of a scholarship— or merely contributing to one's former school to help some struggling student you shall never know. It may be by funding or volunteering at some institution that meets the needs of struggling young people. It may be as a volunteer for a 4H, Little League or Scouting organization. One outlet for Diane and me is the local Food Bank. All my book royalties are donated to them. The thought of children going through the day— or to bed— hungry literally hurts us. Since I enjoy writing, it really costs us nothing. For decades Diane and I participated in the CROP Walks to alleviate world hunger. I even made a CD, "A Preacher Plays Beethoven to Bourbon Street." Everyone won. I enjoyed making it and those who purchased it also enjoyed the music— and thousands of people were helped to provide food for themselves. We sent the $7,000 royalties to CROP. The opportunities to nurture in some way is limited only by your imagination— and genuine interest.

I also never miss the opportunity to teach some eager young would-be-musician how to play the clarinet. I have found such tremendous joy and opportunities from my own clarinet playing, I cannot resist helping anyone so oriented. Most of you have some skill you could share with younger people that would enrich their lives. Diane and I have served as camp counselors, volunteered as short-term missionaries in Guatemala, worked with Epiphany to minister to young people in confinement, led youth groups on tours, and served as volunteer tutors. Those activities are all more satisfying than watching a television rerun. A large number of friendships were developed with people who are kindred spirits.

Although Erikson focuses on empowering the next generation, I include the empowerment of all those who can be helped. Jesus healed the elderly as well as the young. There should be no age limit on assisting others to a more abundant life. I see broken military veterans, hard-working people made homeless by a medical debt, and elderly stored in retirement, abandoned and dying alone. I will never forget a brief time with a reformed alcoholic who had been rescued by the Salvation Army. He had fallen from being a happily married successful realtor with a lovely home in the suburbs, to a divorced, homeless drunk who slept in the streets in the depths of the inner city. Someone literally reached down, took him by the hand and raised him to new life. The Salvation Army practices generativity— and probably thinks nothing of it. It is a natural part of the soul of their organization.

A lovely young woman who had served as a nurse in a children's hospital joined the congregation and immediately expressed an interest in doing something of value. She had become weary of tending dying children and needed a change, but also needed to be of value to others. She noted that many contemporaries were more-or-less homebound because of the need to care for their elderly parents. She came to me with a plan to organize a senior daycare center. Her husband made a very fine salary so she was willing to work as a volunteer in order to get it going. We started in an unused room in the church. Eventually, her daycare took over an abandoned school house and served dozens of families. She turned the center over to competent assistants, and she and her husband loaded a sailboat with medical supplies and hardware (he was a skilled handyman). They sailed to the Amazon where they planned to improve the quality of life for those in the villages along that river. I pray for them and worry for their well-being ... but I never worry about their souls.

Generativity, the simple desire to empower others to enter the world more fully- more successfully, is an attribute every healthy soul must possess.

6. A Passion for Truth

"If you continue in my way you shall come to know the truth and the truth will make you free." John 8:32

You cannot journey elsewhere if you will not leave home. Unless one "hungers and thirsts," in the biblical sense, for truth they never will make a spiritual journey. Far too many who waste their times in biblical studies are like those who watch pictures of foreign lands, but will never journey there, because they consider those places to be unsafe. They may deceive themselves into believing they have acquired some new knowledge, but— in reality— they have only confirmed old, comfortable beliefs. Regardless of what they think of themselves, they are security-oriented and will not abandon comfortable ideas that make them feel secure— regardless of the evidence that they should.

Delusion enslaves the mind. Truth liberates. So much of what passes for religious studies simply is either not true or not relevant. It is neither Biblically-based, nor consistent with the life and teachings of Jesus Christ. Too much of what passes as Christian theology is some secular prejudice or preconceived truth that is masqueraded as Christian thinking. One of the horrible examples was the use of Scripture ("*Slaves obey your masters*" Ephesians 6:5, Colossians 3:22) to justify the enslavement of other humans for personal gain. Uneducated novices tend to equate every word of Scripture at the same level of authority. They learned incorrectly, and pass their ignorance along in good faith that they are doing what is proper. In actuality, however— no matter how fervent and dedicated they may appear, they are damaging and limiting souls, putting them in a false world.

The Books of the Old Testament are the books of the old covenant (The Greek can be translated as either, since they mean the same thing). It is the Jewish Bible that serves as a reference for understanding the Christian Scriptures, but it is not on a par with the books of the New Covenant. Within that framework, we have the words of unknown writers (unknown except for the writings attributed to them). We also have the words and actions attributed to Jesus Christ. Even here, one must be careful. There are certain clear patterns to Jesus words and actions. Those that are attributed to him should be consistent with those patterns. Unfortunately, we have no complete original texts prior to the 4th century of the New Testament writings. Centuries passed before we have anything approximating full copies. During this interval, many pious scribes added their own understandings to the scriptures they copied. This created some errors in early translations such as The King James. This was made from a group of manuscripts with some of the Greek translated from later Latin by a scholar named Erasmus— who sought to read the original Greek.

Any study of Scripture, worthy of being called a genuine study, must draw from contemporary sources of interpretation. New tools are forever being developed that assist the genuine scholar in understanding the meaning behind the words written so long ago, in a foreign culture. The study also must necessarily have some practical everyday focus. There is no point in studying Holy Scripture simply to understand it. The spiritual pilgrims use the lessons of Scripture to formulate plans for their own goals and behavior. The Methodist movement caught fire in England simply because the members of the classes held one another responsible for doing this. It altered their lives, setting them free from old ways of thinking and acting. Jesus' mission was not to deliver information, but to set the people free to live fully as loving, obedient children of a living, ever-present and loving God.

The quest for genuine truth to replace false beliefs and practices must be of paramount concern for the healthy soul.

7. Self-discipline

A healthy soul has adequate self-discipline. Jesus spoke of this when he said, *"No one who puts his hand to the plow and looks back is fit for the kingdom of God."* (Luke 9:62).

Our ability to undertake a radical change is limited. We can only begin and quit a number of times, before we simply lose energy or interest in the project. I have observed this far too many times with smokers and alcoholics. "I gave it a try, but it didn't work for me," is a common excuse for failure. This is one major reason I caution those who feel they are ready to embark on such a venture. A spiritual journey, once begun, is a life-long pilgrimage. There may be resting places along the way, but they are few and far between. The morning prayer for serious spiritual seekers must be some affirmation of their purpose and their dedication to the journey. Jesus told many tales of those who strayed, simply because they had no focus.

Early pilgrims kept journals or diaries to review in order to see any progress or understand their sidetracking. Some of you may wish to try this. I admit, it does not work for me. I am not methodical enough for that. Instead, I use some quiet time in the evening to mentally review the events of the day. I ask myself not only where I might have been more of what I want to be, but why, in some cases, I managed quite well. Critical examination demands we explore both the reasons for failure and for success. After all, it is the successes we strive for. When they occur, what was the difference?

Standard prayer is not for everyone. Some of us do better with a song or hymn. The purpose is to focus upon ourselves as on a journey to spiritual maturity. Any number of hymns fit the bill for that. "*Here I am, Lord. Is it I, Lord? I have heard you calling in the night …*" "*It only takes a spark to get the fire going, but soon all those around can warm up in its glowing. That's how it is with God's love. Once you've experienced it, you spread His love to everyone. You want to pass it on.*"

The possibilities are almost limitless. Start the day with a song in your heart, and the day will go better than if you spent the time, selecting the proper dress or tie.

The healthy soul finds a way to remain focused.

8. Healthy Curiosity

A healthy soul has a healthy interest in the world. It wants to understand how and why things work the way they do. The uninquisitive mind lives (unknowingly, perhaps) in an enclosed vacuum. Acceptance of whatever is, is the rule of the day— the rule of every day. I try to understand my friends— what their lives are like when I am not with them. What guides them? What are their interests? What are their special qualities that attract me? I can nurture those if I understand them. Otherwise, they are come-and-go relationships that actually have no importance to me, aside from my presence with them.

I have done reading on dark energy and dark matter and basic quantum physics. I do not claim to be anywhere near an authority on these, but I do have some basic understanding that gives me an appreciation for the real wonders of this universe God is continually creating. I also enjoy watching episodes of Star Talk, with Neil deGrasse-Tyson. It always is a great exercise in critical thinking.

Most of my friends have avocations or hobbies that satisfy a healthy curiosity about the world. It may be reading, collecting or a number of other avenues of understanding. The point is, that interesting people have a curiosity and a means for satisfying that hunger to know more. The soul, by my definition, determines the quality of your character. You can decide whether a healthy soul is interesting or dull.

One either is open to discovery or closed and satisfied with whatever they now know and or believe. Life is not a status quo experience. Our task on this earth is to acquire understanding.

9. Patience

We all know the standard joke of the person who prays for patience, then ends by checking his watch and adds, *"I'm waiting!"* It fits most of us to some degree, so we chuckle at ourselves when we hear it. The search for a mature and healthy spirituality is a life-long pursuit. There is no point where anyone can say, *"I have arrived."* Some conservatives speak of having been saved. Frankly, I do not know what that entails. The God I serve so joyfully is not a deity I need to fear or be saved from. I believe this will be covered a bit later on when I address the issue of negative vs. positive spirituality.

IN SEARCH OF YOUR SOUL

My original clarinet teacher had the patience of a saint. I was terrible! My tone was poor, my intonation was a mystery, my fingering was incidental— or accidental (either fit). I was only seven years of age and did not quite understand the relationship of the notes printed on the paper and the sound I should be at least expecting. He never yelled, or seemed to lose patience. I recall hearing, "*Oh, Dick, let's try that again,*" dozens (probably hundreds) of times. Without his patience, I never would have matured as a clarinetist, and found such pleasure with the instrument. I try to recall that experience whenever I encounter some situation that requires me to stay calm while another person is struggling to attain some goal.

Raising children ought to be a good patience-building system. They struggle to learn to speak clearly, walk steadily, dress themselves, and take care of the normal bodily requirements in an acceptable manner. Play for them is not only a fun pastime but a learning experience. How does one throw and catch a ball properly? What are the rules for any game? Playing baseball always was an exercise in patience for me. Standing alone in right field, doing nothing, for two or three innings never was my idea of an action game. Still, if I were to fit in and be part of a group I had to learn to do just that. Unfortunately, I have witnessed far too many bridge games where a player has no patience with the partner's errors and hesitations. The old joke, "*Would you like to play a friendly game of cards ... or would you rather play bridge?*" is too real to be humorous. Diane and I had a rule-of-thumb for some couples, in that we never let them play as partners— for fear they might kill one another on the way home. On the other side of the ledger, we also have seen those players who have infinite patience with their partners and rarely— if ever— comment about their mistakes. I think of those persons as healthy souls. The quality of their character shines clearly.

You and I need patience to accomplish anything of lasting value. Relationships develop and strengthen over time. They rarely, if ever, begin looking like in-depth friendships. The song from "The King and I" comes to mind, *"Getting to know you. Getting to know all about you."* Genuine friendships require a level of trust that only experience can build. I easily separate friends from acquaintances. One has expectations of a loyalty in difficult times. The other is superficial and fills the needs of the moment.

There are an endless number of illustrations where patience is the ingredient that turns a possible failure of sorts into a victory. It is the attribute that is required for undertaking any major project— including your spiritual journey.

A healthy soul has patience.

10. Humility

My favorite professor, Albert Sundberg, once shared this little joke with us: *"I once was given a medal for humility ... but I wore it, so they took it away."* My own private joke was to admit. *"I always have been proud of my humility."* Either one makes the point: if you believe you are humble, you probably are not. I sometimes recall a rather bizarre experience from early days with a ministerial fellowship group. One of the clergy used the phrase from Paul: *"Jesus came into the world to save sinners, of whom I am the chief." (1Timothy 1:15)*

Immediately, another clergy actually leaped to his feet and asserted, *"I am the chief sinner!"* Suddenly the entire group engaged in an inverse bidding war— each claiming to be the chief of sinners (that would make them the greatest sinner in the world, incidentally). I sat, fascinated by what was happening. These otherwise sensible men were claiming to be the worst people who lived. I noted that each assertion seemed to convey a sense of superiority while claiming that disreputable title. "What is happening here?" I asked myself. Finally, I realized I was watching almost rabid attempts to be the most humble.

Once I realized this, I lost track of what ensued. Whatever was happening in that room was not something I wanted to share in. I believe I just let my mind wander to a more comfortable place— elsewhere.

By contrast, A noted professor of preaching often was showered with praise during his introduction. He developed a standard way of disarming that. He nodded to the one introducing him and said, *"Thank you for your kind words, but there are no great preachers. There is only one great Lord and Savior, Jesus Christ, and I am privileged to share a few thoughts I have about him today."* There was nothing artificial about this response. The professor was Dr. George Buttrick, who was always listed as one of the top two or three preachers of the early part of the 20th century. George also was the senior editor of the *Interpreters Bible*. Yet, in the classroom and in private, he was a genuinely humble person. He got excited about young authors, and readily acknowledged that his reputation as a senior editor came from the skills of those who wrote the articles— and not himself. I never encountered anyone who had this clarity of understanding of the dynamics of a sermon. His classes always overflowed, even with students from nearby seminaries. He was aware of the gift, and continued to teach well beyond retirement years— not for money (he had enough) but for the service of those who could use his guidance.

I sometimes worry about those individuals who feel the need to boast about themselves. They must be badly in need for some self-assurance. People of talent and high abilities simply do not have to tell others they are special. If we cannot recognize that a person is special, it probably is because that person is *not* special. A tall person does not have to wear a sign saying he is tall. We recognize it. A person graced with physical beauty does not have to wear a beauty crown. We recognize the beauty. A person of high intelligence does not have to wear a sign displaying his or her IQ. We recognize a superior intellect when we encounter it. And so it goes. So, when a person obviously feels the need to place themselves in some to-be-admired position, I have to wonder how bad their need is.

To me, genuine humility has nothing to do with a lack of self-confidence or meekness of any kind. It simply is a self-recognition that we all are pretty much the same. I excel in some areas, but am quite inept in others. I do well in the classroom, but not so well in the shop or laboratory. I play the clarinet well, but was never more than mediocre on the saxophone. I sometimes chuckle, remembering an observation by Garrison Keeler. "*Many people have musical talent ... but not so many as believe they have.*" Hopefully, we all do a few things reasonably well, but if the term average is to have any meaning, that is where most of us find ourselves most of the time.

The humble people I know and admire are self-confident. Experience has taught them that they can produce or accomplish what is required to succeed. They simply believe that this skill does not set them apart from ordinary people. They do not deserve special attention or privileges.

Genuine humility allows one to accept whatever gifts cause him or her to be recognized and admired, but these gifts also are viewed as an obligation. God has given you certain gifts, that are to be used in such a way as to enhance the quality of life for yourself and others. A genuinely humble individual accepts this with appreciation, not arrogance.

Developing a Healthy Soul

What does it require to develop healthy soul? Athletic trainers know the secret to developing a healthy body. It is a combination of activities that ultimately becomes a life-style. One cannot go on a diet and become healthy. It involves a disciplined, balanced style of eating, exercise, and sleeping. It is not an "either/or" choice. The same is true of developing a healthy soul: it requires a disciplined, balanced set of activities. As with a healthy body, that life-style must continue throughout your life. Jesus spoke of those who cannot finish the course— who fell short of becoming genuine spiritual pilgrims. He did not state the reasons, for there were too many. He merely cautioned those who wanted to become his followers (Luke 14:28-33). Count the cost and decide if you can pay it before you start to develop a healthy soul. It requires work— disciplined work— over the years.

When I was quite young I made the decision to play the clarinet. I wanted to play it well enough to find genuine enjoyment from doing so. I studied with the best teacher in the area, and practiced at least two hours every day. In 9th grade I was first chair solo in the high school band. The next year I was first chair solo in the all—state band. Now in my 80's I still play in the church orchestra and a small jazz combo. People often say they wish they had my talent. I flunked the first semester in clarinet at school. All I had was desire and discipline— nothing more. It takes no special talent to have a healthy soul— just desire and discipline. Think about it.

DR. RICHARD CHEATHAM

Just as anyone pursuing a healthy body has certain talents and interests, so we all have special talents and interests in the realm of our souls. The Hindu religion recognizes those differences, and has designed four different disciplines (yogas) for spiritual growth.

- Raja Yoga is for the meditative person.
- Jnana Yoga is for the rational *person*.
- Bhakti Yoga is for those who respond strongly to emotions such as love.
- Karma Yoga is for those who prefer physical action to reading or reflecting.

As you read this brief list of methods for spiritual nurture, one or more may particularly appeal to you. Feel free to tailor your own method to fit you. Each ingredient is important and should be included, but you decide the balance. Remember, you will be creating a life-long life style.

Do remember that empathy is the essential foundation. In his parable about a final judgment, separating the sheep from the goats, Jesus emphasizes the importance of empathy: those who relate strongly to others who are in need, also are spiritually related to God. Those who can ignore the needs of others are spiritually separated (Matthew 25:31-46). In every human encounter, we should pause long enough to realize we are speaking with a person whose personal history is different from ours, but who shares all the needs and desires. Whenever you watch a performer, remember that person is as human as yourself. Before you become critical, ask yourself if you could pay the emotional cost of publically performing. You might even try imagining what is happening in the performers mind. I have acted, sung and played my clarinet publically and know I always feel some anxieties or concerns: Will I forget my lines? What if my voice cracks or the clarinet reed is too dry, or I stray off key? (I have experienced all those and more, incidentally). Remember the person is doing the best she/he can at that moment. I have seen comedians slowly die in front of an audience, as they realize (from the lack of laughter) that their material is not entertaining. I hurt with them as I think of how I would feel in their situation. It always is painful for me. In the same way, I quietly rejoice when some unknown comedian does well when showcased on an evening TV show.

When an acquaintance stumbles her/his way through relating an incidence, have patience and quietly encourage them with affirming comments— or grunts. Not everyone can tell a story well. Your acquaintance is doing her/his best. When you read of a tragedy that occurred in some remote place, think of the people as distant friends. They are fellow humans who have been severely hurt and, perhaps, saddened. Take a moment to quietly pray for them.

Reading is essential. I caution about reading the Bible as a spiritual discipline. Much of the Old Testament is history— often distorted by the bias of the author. Most of the New Testament books are worthy. At seminary, my New Testament professor spent one hour on the Book of Revelation. He explained that this was a style of writing that gave the writer some protection against being accused of treason for criticizing the government. It overflows with symbolism that made sense to those who read it at the time, but confuses the contemporary Scripturally uneducated today. The Eastern Church does not claim it as authoritative.

For me, the synoptic Gospels are golden. You need to know that both Luke and Matthew used Mark as their outline and added what they learned from other sources. Neither of them had ever known Jesus. Still, they add to his teachings and his actions, without which we would be impoverished. I would suggest you read the likes of a Marcus Borg who used contemporary scholarship techniques to present a clearer, more genuine understanding of our faith. An early book of mine, *Can You Make the Buttons Even?* Relates much of my own spiritual pilgrimage.

Develop a disciplined method for your reading. It might be one evening per week or every evening. Experiment to see what fits you. Do not worry if the routine is interrupted, or if you feel the need to change after trying it a while.

Another indispensable activity is silence. I resonate to words from the introduction to the song, "You Raise Me Up." "... *then I am still, and wait here in the silence, until you come and sit awhile with me."* I first encountered God as I sat in silence, contemplating His existence in my life. I was completely engulfed in a Presense that filled my being with a sense of serenity, acceptance and love. I still make a regular practice of finding silent time during the day, to merely sit in His Presence. Some of you may have difficulty in sensing the Presence. We all have varying degrees of awareness to different realities. My sense of smell is poor; my sense of taste is mediocre at best. Some people have exquisite sense of smell and taste and earn their livelihood as testers. Some of us are more aware of the presence of another. Still, whatever your gift in this area, use a time of silence to contemplate the Presence of the Divine in your life. God is an ever-present reality in your life. He speaks to you through your soul. When you learn to heed the messages— in whatever form they appear— your soul will be nourished.

A Christian actively practices the faith— not just by worship or involvement in church activities. The earliest term for a congregation was *ekklesia*, from which we derive the term ecclesiastical. The term literally means "called out." Christians were the ones called out by God to be ambassadors of reconciliation (II Corinthians 5:17-20). The extent of your actions will be limited only by your imagination, health and resources. I know some elderly persons whose ministry is a morning call to other seniors— who are alone. There are short-term mission ventures, lasting a week or more. There are some great ongoing opportunities offered by many congregations. Stephen Ministry is rewarding for all I know who became one. Emmaus Walk and Epiphany (a ministry to imprisoned teenagers) are others that I personally have found to be rewarding. Hospitals can always use volunteers. Many schools welcome additional help from volunteers. Some congregations have organized prayer groups who pray for needy members. The lovers can employ any of these as opportunities. As I said, the possibilities are only limited *by you.*

Negative vs. Positive Theologies

All ideas are based on assumed premises. I set forth my two essential premises in formulating any concept of the healthy soul: a doctrine of God and a doctrine of humanity.

Typical Christians seem to alternate in their understanding of God as either one of unconditional love, or of judgment. Their choice appears to rest upon their mood of the moment. If someone they do not know commits a horrendous act, their God of judgment is invoked, hoping the perpetrator will be struck down or at least consigned to Hell. However, if the same act is committed by someone known and/or cared for, then the God of unconditional love is invoked, and a prayer for forgiveness and redemption is offered.

I believe a careful, thoughtful reading of the Gospel accounts suggest that any judgment is the natural consequence of one's actions. Although Jesus appears to set forth a place of judgement, it seems evident that he merely is expressing the consequences of one's selfish actions. Separation from God is not being condemned to exile, but is the natural result of withdrawing from the Presence of God in one's life. The judgment expressed in Matthew 27 is both positive and negative. Those who extended themselves for the well-being of another were in sync with God's will. Those whose egocentricity caused them to ignore the cries of need have effectively removed themselves from God's will, and have stepped outside of His Kingdom. It is a metaphor—

really that simple. One should not attempt to make it a literal event waiting in the future.

The parable we call "The Prodigal Son," but was more correctly renamed, "The Waiting Father," by Helmut Thielicke is Jesus' depiction of the nature of God as a loving parent. The son has intentionally left home and wasted his inheritance. He then returns— not because he misses the family or is in any way regretful of what he has done. He returns home out of necessity, because life apart from the family has defeated him. He is weary and hungry and realized his parent's servants live better. When the father observes his son returning, he stops what he is doing and rushes to greet him. There are no recriminations— only joy and relief that a lost son has returned home. The father calls for a celebration so that others might share in his joy.

The later doctrine of atonement was conceived by good people who inserted their own values into the thinking of the church. The notion that humans are essentially sinners in need of redemption is not in the teachings of Jesus. There is a vague reference in Matthew 26:28 when Jesus seems to suggest that his blood is shed for the forgiveness of sins. However, any reputable biblical scholar understands that Matthew is copying from the Gospel of Mark— that omits this phrase— as does Luke, who also is using Mark as a framework for his own manuscript. Additionally, no 1st or 2nd century manuscript of Matthew exists, so this well may be an addition by some pious scribe who thought he was being helpful. There was a great deal of that type of material that had to be cleaned up before reliable translations were available.

The serious spiritual pilgrim must make some rational decision about the nature of God and humanity. God is either a judge, willing to condemn his creatures to an eternity of punishment for their behavior during their brief stay on earth, or God is a loving parent who nourishes and guides his children.

Everything I know about Jesus affirms the latter.

In that regard, humanity must be viewed as either essentially sinful in need of redemption, or as a child of God who uses the time on earth to mature properly. Jesus tells relative strangers they are the light of the world, and calls them to let that light shine. He tells them God is their heavenly father, thereby implying they are God's children— as Scripture says, "made in His image." He does tell egocentric Pharisees that they are sinners for their behavior, but never implies that is their nature.

Rather than using the customary terms of *liberal* and *conservative*, I choose to use *"positive"* and *"negative'* to distinguish what I view as the two major divisions in Christianity. We tend to take some orientations for granted, tacitly assuming them to be eternal truths. Novice travelers often are shocked to discover the cultural differences that abound around the world. I recall studying some cultural anthropologists who described a culture that was structured on guilt and indebtedness. Another was structured around generosity and sharing. With just those two, you might see where I am heading on my identification as either negative or positive. Sigmund Freud and Carl Jung broke their relationship over this issue. Freud tended to view psychology through a premise of pathology, where Jung saw it as a tool for maturity. The Western Christian church, under the guidance of such theologians as Augustine and Calvin, emphasize the sinfulness of humanity and claim Jesus died on the cross in atonement for our sins. The Eastern church, however, has no doctrine of atonement, and views humanity as being in the image of God, and requires nurture and guidance to become the fullness of that image. When I read the teachings and statements attributed to Jesus, I find little support for the negative theology, and an abundance of support for the positive theology. Nowhere do I find even a hint that God is angry with— or alienated from— humanity. The parable of the workers in the vineyard who receive the same pay, no matter when they began to work, speaks of a loving deity who welcomes any who want to be a part of his Kingdom.

My intent in writing this is to strip Jesus' message of its traditional form and analyze the underlying dynamics of the development of our souls. A simple psychological truth that every teacher, preacher and— yes— parent ought to know is this:

We do not become what others call us to become,
but we tend to become what others say we are.

I want you to imagine being raised in a negative household. When you step into the kitchen for breakfast, you are greeted with a question like this: "Did you clean up your room or leave it like the mess you usually do?" When you leave for school, you are told, "Try to behave today and not mess up too badly. When you return, you are asked where you failed to be at your best. At Sunday supper, everyone at the table repeats a printed prayer that goes like this:

"Lord, we have failed to live like a good family should. We have not listened to one another nor helped one another when they needed our help. We have not been good neighbors or members of the community. We have not done our share to make the community a better place. We have not done all the decent, helpful things we know we should have done. Forgive us, we pray and help guide and empower us to be better in the future. Amen"

By the time you were fifteen you ether would have left home, decided to wait patiently to leave when you graduate, or accepted the fact that you are a failure.

Now envision being raised in a positive household. When you step into the kitchen you are greeted with a, *"Good morning! I hope you slept well."* When you leave for school you are reminded *"God has given you wonderful potentials, and school can help you develop them. Enjoy your classes and classmates— and make it a good day for yourself and for them."*

The Sunday dinner prayer follows this pattern: *"Lord, we thank you for this loving family and the fine community in which we live. We know we have much to learn. Each of us has our struggle to become what you call us to be, but we are grateful for what life-in-Thee has taught us thus far. Guide and empower us to live in the example of Jesus that we may walk in the path that leads us ever closer to Thee. Amen"*

If we are fortunate, we have parents who recognize we have much to learn in order to become worthy, self-actuating adults, but still affirm us, lead us by precept and example, guide us into becoming— not what they want us to be— but what we choose to become, utilizing the gifts we have been given.

Jesus did not come to revitalize or start a new religion. He came to show and assure us that our Creator God was that kind of a parent. He taught by precept and example the kind of life we should live in order to be in proper relationship with that heavenly parent, and be able to live our lives fully and worthily— with no fear of what was to follow.

Through my studies of church history— and daily observations— I have watched the church lose its way time and time again, simply because it lost sight of the simplicity of Jesus' mission and message. Affirm and accept God's love and care for each of you, draw from the power of his spirit that resides within you, combat the evil destructive powers of this world, care for those in need. Allow yourself to be transformed from your egocentricity to a person of genuine compassion and empathy with others— and in doing so, become one who lives under the reign and rule of God and not the Caesars of society.

Now place this analogy in the settings of a church and you can understand the dilemma we face. The so-called moderate church is losing members at a steady rate. They bought into the Calvinist doctrine of humanity as essentially sinners in need of redemption. Jesus is placed in the role of sacrificial lamb while the members are passive recipients of his grace.

There was no spirit of negativity in the early church. Rather there was a spirit of affirmation— that lifted people to become what God called them to become. Whoever came up with the notion that Jesus had to die in atonement for our sins before God could be reconciled to us certainly had not even found a suggestion of that in Scripture Whoever it was, was drawing from his own limited experience. His failure to properly utilize the written records started the Church on a false— and I believe: destructive— path.

In Matthew 5:13 Jesus tells his listeners, *"You are the salt of the earth."* That is the proper message for Christ's followers.

In Matthew 18:12-14, Jesus tells the parable of the shepherd who went in search of his one lost sheep. He concludes by saying, *"In the same way, your Father in heaven is not willing that one of these little ones be lost."*

Paul obviously grasped this message. His introduction in his various letters testify to that.

Romans 1:7
*To all in Rome who are loved by God
and called to be saints.*

I Corinthians 1:2
*To the church of God in Corinth, to those sanctified
in Christ Jesus and called to be holy.*

II Cornithians1:1
*To the church of God in Corinth, together
with all the saints throughout Achaia.*

DR. RICHARD CHEATHAM

Ephesians 1:1
*To the saints in Ephesus,
the faithful in Christ Jesus.*

Philippians 1:1
To all the saints in Christ Jesus in Philippi.

You may be wondering how we ever perverted the message to such negativity as we now have. I did, and that is one reason I pursued a doctorate in Church History. I was able to read early manuscripts in their original languages, and to study a variety of writings by the early leaders who shaped our doctrines. Essentially, these people ignored the guidance offered by Scripture. They drew from their own experience and values— and by doing so— set the church on the wrong path. The books of the New Testament were not declared authoritative until 383A.D., so this is understandable. However, the results are that the Church has been operating with a negative message instead of the affirming one offered by Jesus.

Most of us suffer feelings of guilt on occasion. We stumble through much of our lives, finding our way, and are so self-involved that we overlook the needs and rights of others. St. Augustine, a 5th century bishop was particularly troubled by guilt. His *Confessions* is a classic. He had a powerful mind, and added some good thoughts to our faith, but in my opinion, his contribution toward making guilt a central factor more than offset his positive contributions. He clearly formulated the doctrine of Original Sin. This is the teaching that Adam's Fall in some way infected all humanity. Paul had some of this floating around in him, but it was Augustine that set it in stone, so to speak.

This totally contradicts the 18th chapter of Ezekiel. In that chapter, Ezekiel, as a spokesman for God (*prophet* means spokesperson, not a predictor) clearly says that neither the sins nor the righteousness of a parent is passed to children.

The Jewish faith, though it had a day of atonement, had no doctrine of Original Sin. The Atonement was for the sins committed during the year. Any reflective theologian understands that Jesus would not die for atonement for what Adam did. There is a throw-away line in Matthew's version of the last supper, "for the forgiveness of sins," that is used for justification. However, we have no 1st or 2nd century editions of Matthew. This well may have been added later. Mark which was the primary source— and provided the outline— for Matthew and Luke makes no mention of it. Records of the early celebration of the Eucharist (Giving-of-thanks) make no mention of it. The doctrine of Atonement never — *never*— was accepted or certified by any church council. Still, it has become central in far too many churches. Our hymnals reek of it. "Jesus died for my sins," or "Jesus our Savior" are too-common themes.

For a moment, I want to explore the idea of us humans as sinners from a different angle. As humans, we have an essential nature. Most of the present churches say it is as *sinner*. I believe I have made the case that this is not what Jesus called us. Genesis tells us we are made in the image of God. Jesus told us to call God "*Father*." This term implies that we are Children-of-God. I believe I also made the case that nothing in the New Testament writings suggest God feels alienated from us.

We do not know where the earlier tale was written. Most scholars assume it was in an arid place, where life was difficult. The second was written in Babylon, a few centuries later where there was an abundance of water, and life was easier. The writers were in exile and apparently wished to affirm the basic goodness of creation.

Looking Beyond

Ultimately, the purpose of this life-on-earth is to fashion your soul in a manner that prepares you for eternity. The soul is that nebulous eternal portion of our being that is you, unencumbered by the ego. Your soul is, in fact, the essence of who you are. When the soul is manifested in the personality it is the quality we call *character*. Carl Jung called it "The Self" or the *"Imago Dei."* (*Image of God*). For him, it represented the human potential to actually become as God.

This model, for me, assumes a form of reincarnation. There are those who claim that the idea of reincarnation is a heresy. That idea was proposed at the Council of 553 A.D. Until that time, it was an accepted doctrine of the church. The idea of an eternal place of bliss called "Heaven" is non-biblical and developed later.

Reincarnation is the best understanding that allows continual development of the human soul. A place of eternal bliss would not be conducive to soul development. Conflict and struggle are essential ingredients for that to occur. Personally, I believe I am a long way from being what God had in mind when he began creating humanity. I am far too petty, to self-occupied, too wasteful of time and my many resources, and add a multitude of other short-comings— to be what my heavenly father wishes for me— and all those I know— to become ... and remain at that level through eternity. I believe we were made to be companions of God. I resonate to Robert Johnson's Genesis poem, "And God said, *'I'm lonely. I think I will make myself a world.'*" If God's nature is to love, then God needs someone— or many someones— to love.

We know that every new-born child emerges with a quality of personality. Some are active and noisy, while others are quiet and passive. Every parent has learned that each child must be treated differently. What works for one does not necessarily work for another. We even refer to some young children as being "old souls." They seem to possess a quality of wisdom that is beyond what should be expected. Others may be naive and gullible. What has been born is a soul, with memory erased, but with the qualities of being that have been developed by previous lives— intact.

I am not one who believes in either heaven or hell. Either one demeans God. My God is too large for such pettiness. The idea that our few years on this planet Earth would determine an eternity of either reward or punishment diminishes a Creator God whose universe extends 14 billion light years and is still expanding. The minuscule deity who sat on a mountain when we thought the world was 4000 years old and the Earth was the center of the universe simply cannot exist in our mind today. We have gone far beyond that— and if we have not— then shame on us. We have sacrificed our intellectual capacity for reasoning in order to remain complacent and comfortable in a childish belief system.

I believe it is the soul (our true Self) that continues beyond our life-on-Earth. The mind is a portion and function of the soul, and I believe it resides within us during a time of denouement. I believe there will be a time of reunion with those who have gone before us. There also will be an important time of debriefing when we are made to realize the lessons we learned by our time on earth —and how much more we still need to learn. Eternity will not be experienced in the realm of time and space as we presently understand it. Einstein demonstrated that both time and space have no absolute value. They exist in order for material things to exist. Both time and space alter in their dimension depending upon the speed of the material thing that resides in that realm. When you remove the material things there is no reason for either time nor space to exist. I believe that was the condition before the Big Bang. Prior to that, there was only the nonphysical— the spiritual. In the spiritual realm, all relationships will be spiritual. I have no idea what this will be like, for my brain— like yours— developed and evolved in the realm of time and space, and we simply are not wired to be able to comprehend this realm of the spirit. I only can assume it must exist. "God is spirit," Jesus said. That's good enough for me. It has to be.

I believe we must grow spiritually far beyond what we now are, in order to dwell in that realm for a lengthy time. That is why I postulate a doctrine of reincarnation as part of the maturing process. The Earth is a marvelous place for spiritual growth. There is order, yet uncertainty. There is— for most people— a constant need to do work of some kind in order to survive.

The early church had a doctrine of reincarnation that was affirmed in the Council of 451A.D. That was dismissed under the influence of Empress Theodora, wife of Justinian, in the 6th century. Prior to that time, reincarnation was a vital part of Christian theology. In that respect, it was similar to the great religions of Hinduism and Buddhism. Humanity continued to evolve through eternity, ultimately arriving at the state of pure spiritual bliss. The Council of 451A.D. reaffirmed this. However, Theodora was a scheming, self-centered woman who desired to be worshipped as a deity, as the earlier Caesars had been. She had been born a commoner, but was quite lovely and gained fame and fortune as a prostitute. She eventually became part of Justinian' harem, then— ultimately— his wife. She realized that she could not be worshipped as a goddess if she were to be reincarnated. She schemed with religious figures who apparently realized that their product of eternal bliss was meaningless if reincarnation actually occurred. Finally, at the Council of 531 reincarnation was condemned as a heresy.

The ego does not begin to develop for the first two years, so the soul is vulnerable and influenced by whatever occurs. This is a primary reason that the first two— three years are properly managed by parents. Erik Erikson observes that the earliest necessary quality be of a basic trust— as opposed to distrust. This is the foundation upon which the entire life shall rest. I believe the great tragedy of Richard Nixon's life was that it was built upon a foundation of distrust. If one reads of his early childhood, it is easy to understand how that occurred. This distrust led him astray and eventually destroyed his presidency. By contrast, we may look at the life of Helen Keller, who was totally dependent upon the care of others. She lived a life of optimism and contentment. We know this is the time when much self-doubt develops, and also when many champions begin their journey of achievement. Because of our strong Calvinist heritage, much guilt is spread on children, like fertilizer that will, unfortunately, nourish their souls throughout their lives. A wise parent knows better than to use guilt as a motivating factor. However, "the sins of the parents are visited to the children" so these debilitating practices are unthinkingly passed from generation to generation.

A healthy, well-developed soul, utilizing the essential soul that was born, will be equipped to do well on this leg of its eternal journey. It will be able to learn the lessons for which it was born, and leave the world richer and better for its having lived.

Modern American religion has proven to be of little— if any— assistance in nurturing the soul and connecting to the ego. Many of the conservative element may think of themselves as spiritual, but their faith is primarily political and repressive. Where Jesus was lovingly accepting, they are negatively judgmental. Where Jesus was liberating, they are repressive ("Co*ntinue in my way and you will know the truth and* *the truth will set you free."* John 8:32). It develops personalities that seem antithetical to Jesus Christ. Much of what passes for the more liberal aspects of religion is more akin to dabbling than a pilgrimage. It may instill a strong moral-ethical foundation, but ignores the spiritual dimension that would cause those qualities to be a natural fruit of the personality. "Shoulds", and "oughts" are key words. Although, in fairness, I readily acknowledge there are many saints whose spirits are rich and productive in the work of God's Kingdom. They may arise from any part of the religious spectrum.

Finally, I must acknowledge another possibility. There may come a time when God simply writes us off as a failure. If we never mature spiritually, and go through every life cycle in loneliness and discontent, God in His mercy may simply give us "The peace that passes all understanding." We simply cease to be: oblivion ... We will have failed God and ourselves, so— like the seeds that are sown but never flourish, we, too, will disappear from the scene. It will not be painful. God does not punish us for who we are. We simply will cease to be.

The Jesus Movement

I noted that Jesus did not intend to start a new religion. He never preached, and obviously did not spend time in public prayer. His close followers even had to ask him how to pray, and he gave only a cursory response. Jesus' mission was to teach people how to live in close relationship to God. In doing so, he believed, the soul would dominate the ego and people would live worthy, fulfilling lives in peaceful, loving, supportive communities. His teachings and his actions were the message. For a variety of reasons, the church lost the original meaning of his mission and developed far lesser ones that have too often manifested itself in corruption and waste.

An early theologian named Tertulian referred to the faith as a *philosophy*. A philosophy defines a lifestyle. It has no religious overtones. Tertullian recognized the power and uniqueness of the Jesus movement, and quickly became a part of it. The great Greek philosophers, Socrates, Plato and Aristotle set forth philosophies their adherents adopted and followed. There was no need for worship. Jesus saw none and proclaimed none. His primary concern was in presenting a philosophy or lifestyle that was grounded in the love and will of God. It was the misunderstandings and needs of followers that converted this newly-proclaimed philosophy into a religion. To help understand this, we should remember that the Jewish culture was essentially a religious culture. The law was derived from the covenant made with Moses. Matthew obviously perceived Jesus as a new Moses. He gives him the miraculous escape from danger, and sends him to Egypt, that he might leave Egypt to redeem the world. Jesus does not set forth a list of rules, as did Moses, but he has him define and redefine them in his Sermon on the Mount. They become rules-of-thumb to be followed by the faithful.

The first century understanding of the physical world was vastly different from what is commonly believed today. Gods were anthropomorphic— and some took earth-bound humans as mates to produce a demigod. Hercules and Bacchus were sons of Jupiter by different mothers. Remus and Romulus, co-founders of Rome, were considered to be twin sons of Mars, by an earthly mother. It would not require much imagination to believe that one risen from the dead, also must be at least a son of deity. If you pay any attention to the birth narratives in Matthew and Luke, you must realize they are mutually exclusive. Both cannot be true. In Luke, Joseph and Mary travel from Nazareth to Bethlehem for a census and tax that actually never occurred (the attempt collapsed at the start because of resistance). Had it actually occurred, it would not have called for men to return to the village of their birth. No birth records were kept, and it would have created chaos, uprooting thousands from their homes and sending them to where there were no facilities for them. Matthew has Joseph and Mary in Bethlehem from the beginning, and the magi find them in a home a year or so later. I would note that the thought of a star moving as a guide, or stopping directly over a house is absurd. It may have seemed likely in the small universe known by the 1st century. However, in our vast universe with the stars being light years away, a star overhead appears directly overhead to a vast number of people.

Having debunked the historicity of the birth narratives, I readily admit that I believe them to be mythically true. Remember that the purpose of a myth is to convey an idea that is too large for ordinary language. As with the wonderful Creation myth in Genesis 1, it does not have to be factual.

Genesis 1 affirmed the goodness of Creation for the exiles in Babylon. The birth myths convey the understanding of a messiah who was unwanted, feared by the powerful power-hungry, and cherished by the outcasts and marginal ones (shepherds fell in that category). As an adult, Jesus, himself, proclaimed that the son of man had no place to lay his head. (Matthew 8:20, Luke 9:58). Every Christmas season I sing "O Little Town of Bethlehem," with belief in my heart. ("Where meek souls shall receive him still, the dear Christ enters in.").

Some unknown pious scribe added "Son of God" to his introduction of Mark and created the false impression that Peter saw Jesus as divine. That error has been discovered and corrected in more recent translations. Otherwise, it is obvious that Peter perceived Jesus as a spirit-filled human—nothing more (Mark, incidentally, is understood to be the memoirs of Peter his uncle).

The Gospel of John presents a radically different view of Jesus from Mark and the other two synoptic gospels. Where Mark shows Jesus attempting to keep his powers secret, John practically has him wearing a sweatshirt proclaiming his divinity.

The introduction states that Jesus is the divine *Logos* incarnate. Translators use the term "Word" to denote *Logos*. This only serves to confuse those uniformed of the meaning of *Logos*. We have no counterpart in our culture. *Logos* was the term that denoted the underlying structure that gave substance to a word. The divine *Logos* was a Stoic concept. It was all quite speculative and no one accepts that concept today. However, we Christians are stuck with it. When outsiders began to accuse Christians of worshipping more than one deity agile theologians latched onto the term *Logos* and shaped it into the Nicene Creed, which few clergy can explain.

Jesus never makes a claim at equality with God. *Jesus said to him, "Have I been with you so long, and you still do not know me,*

Philip? Whoever has seen me has seen the Father. How can you say, 'Show us the Father?' Do you not believe that I am in the Father and the Father is in me? The words that I say to you I do not speak on my own authority, but the Father who dwells in me does his works." (John 14:9-10).

To say, "the Father who dwells in me," does not begin to suggest one that is of the same essence as the Father.

Mark refers to the miracles as "powers" (Greek *dunamus*). John calls them *signs*. Even with that, it is the introduction that proclaims Jesus as the Word Incarnate. In the Gospel, Jesus even says, *"The Father is greater than I."* (John 14:28). A mistranslation of the 1:5 has caused us to misunderstand John's essential message. The traditional interpretations say, *"The light shines in the darkness and the darkness has not overcome it."* Continuing studies have discovered that the term "overcome" actually means what the Greek says: "The darkness *has not grasped it"* Pious translators thought that to not grasp it was the equivalent of not overcoming. However, it meant the same that it does in English: to not grasp something is to not understand it. This is reaffirmed in verse 9-10: *"The true light that gives light to everyone was coming into the world, He was in the world, and though the world was made through him, the world did not recognize him."* Nicodemus did not "get it." The Pharisees did not "get it." The high priests did not "get it." The common people did not "get it," and even called for his crucifixion. Luke 23:34 has the same theme: *"Forgive them, Father, for they know not what they do."* Matthew 23:37 *and Luke 13:34* both cite Jesus as saying Jerusalem kills its prophets.

I interpret this to mean that the people were operating out of their ego— disconnected from their soul. Poor Nicodemus could not begin to understand what Jesus was saying. His mind was grounded in the legalism of the faith. Legalism is a product of the ego— never the soul. He was in touch enough, however, to realize Jesus had a message worthy of learning. He obviously hung around and was there to bury Jesus after his crucifixion. Jesus had promised that *"If you continue in my way you will know the truth."* (John 8:32) Nicodemus continued and finally was free enough to act on behalf of one slain by Roman Law (John 19:38-42).

Many times, I have used a sport anecdote to illustrate my sermons. Inevitably, someone will depart and share a similar sport anecdote with me. I always smile and nod my head in agreement. However, I ache a bit inside because I realize the person has been listening with his ego and I was trying to speak to his soul. We had acted out the dialogue between Nicodemus and Jesus.

Paul grasped the issue and shared it as part of his message. In Roman 12:2 he writes *"Do not conform to the pattern of this world, but be transformed by the renewing of your mind. Then you will be able to test and approve what God's will is—his good, pleasing and perfect will."* We could write that as do not let your ego be the dominant force of your mind. Listen and reason with your soul, and you will be more in touch and in tune with God's will *for your life*. Far too many pew sitters only hear what their ego allows them to hear. They may feel uplifted— even inspired by a sermon -, but they do not dig beneath the surface words to understand. I sometimes fondly recall a member who was dean of one of the engineering schools at the University of Michigan. He told me he would begin to ponder my sermon on the Sunday afternoon (in the spare moments he had). Usually, along about Wednesday he would say to himself, *"That is what he meant.!"* He grasped the spiritual truths I was trying to convey.

Long ago I became aware that the most effective way to profit from studying Scriptures is to relate to the characters you read about. `I am the Pharisee, the prodigal son and older brother, the leper, the blind and crippled. Only then do I grasp the truths expressed.

As I reflect upon the events of the 50's through the 70's I must admit that we in America do the same. The voices that called for justice and equality were violently silenced. For me, this is further evidence of our disconnect between our souls and our egos.

The early Christians formed socialistic communities where they held all things in common (Acts 2:44, 4:32). They saw their mission as creating a loving community and caring for those in need. As they became more Roman this changed. Over a long period, the focus changed from caring for others to "being saved." This radically redefined the faith. Those who claimed the power to forgive became quite powerful. They proclaimed they held the keys to heaven and only those they blessed could enter. If you believe this, then the person with that power has great power over everyone. The early church history tells many conflicts between the civil and ecclesiastical authorities over this issue. With the collapse of Rome, however, the field was open to clergy alone and they took advantage of it. Those who opposed them would be excommunicated— cast out into eternal darkness. During this time, the remnants of the original faith were maintained essentially in monasteries and nunneries. Also, there were the faithful priests who cared less for earthly goods than for the well-being of those entrusted to their care.

Conclusion

I realize this has been a conglomeration of ideas. The soul is not a neat package that can be easily examined or explained. It is the essence of who we are in all our complexity. The development of this is our primary purpose on this earth. Many— perhaps most— get lost along the way and allow themselves to be guided entirely by their ego. They may seemingly acquire a measure of success by those standards. However, for all intents and purposes, they have wasted the opportunity this lifetime offered them.

This vast universe is designed, created and maintained by a source far too complex for us to grasp. It is not being done for us— but *with us* and other intelligent life-forms as key ingredients. We only have bits and snatches of information to determine our purpose. I mentioned earlier that there are— and have been— people who seem to possess a special understanding of the spiritual realm. We call them prophets. When all is said and done, those writings we call Holy Scripture only have authority from the prophets of whom they speak. The New Testament has its ultimate authority in the Gospel accounts— but only if you understand their origin. The letters and others are only commentaries made by time-bound humans.

With Jesus as the paramount guide, we who call ourselves Christians have the option to understand and apply his teachings, or to rationalize them to fit our own short-term goals. Far too much of this is occurring in the faith, and Christianity as a vital shaping force for society and individuals is fading in our culture. As I said at the beginning of this, the disconnect between our ego and our soul is revealing itself in a crumbling culture where selfishness, dishonesty and crudeness are becoming common and acceptable.

A healthy, connected soul is achievable for all who genuinely desire to live in a closer relationship with our loving Heavenly Father. A healthy, connected soul creates those blessed (or fortunate) ones of whom Jesus speaks in The Sermon on the Mount. It creates a life that is more content, more optimistic, less fearful, and more accepting of reality.

When we have developed healthy souls, whatever lies ahead will be to our advantage. Further, we will have fulfilled the purpose for which we have been created. We will be complete. I hope this has been of help to you in giving you some understandings to develop your soul to the fullest.

Richard Cheatham
January 6, 2019

SOURCE
POWER
BEING

Other Books by
DR. RICHARD CHEATHAM

Can You Make the Buttons Even?

* * *

The God Makers

* * *

The Pilgrim Messiah

* * *

Following Jesus Beyond Traditional Christianity

* * *

Special Blessings

* * *

Rediscovering Christianity

CPSIA information can be obtained
at www.ICGtesting.com
Printed in the USA
LVHW040214280519
619246LV00002B/282/P